PRAISE FOR LINE PAPIN

"A fable, a dream, a nightmare, Line Papin's sharp little book fits like a wedge between the ribs. Her tale, remarkably wise from one her age, is a perfect illustration of nostalgia as a homesickness so severe one can die of it, and Papin nearly does, transplanted from the warmth of family intimacy in Việt Nam to the bewildering grayness of France. In the end, her journey reveals itself to be a love story: for the past, for childhood, and for Hà Nội, but also, hopefully, for herself."

—VIẾT THANH NGUYỄN, PULITZER-PRIZE WINNING AUTHOR OF *THE SYMPATHIZER*

"[I]mpressive... [Line Papin's work has] magnificent pages on Hanoi, its humid, deleterious atmosphere where life and death cohabit as if in the same aquarium, its perpetual torpor and excitement... [Her writing] is poetic and romantic."

—ANNIE ERNAUX, NOBEL-PRIZE WINNING AUTHOR OF *GETTING LOST*

"After a remarkable debut, Line Papin chooses the intimate as raw material and delivers. Her account is inhabited by the voice of her elders, but also by a visceral need to narrate herself in order to reconcile with herself. Her writing... remains bewitching and singular."

— *ELLE* (FRANCE)

The GIRL BEFORE HER

Published by Ink & Blood (an imprint of Kaya Press)
Printed in the United States
26 25 24 23 4 3 2 1

Distributed by D.A.P./Distributed Art Publishers // artbook.com (800) 388-BOOK
ISBN: 978-1-885030-83-2
Library of Congress Control Number: 2023933082

Cover artwork by Diana Nguyễn // www.diananguyen.ca
Book design by spoon+fork // www.spoonandforkstudio.com

The Ink & Blood imprint would never have existed without the visionary advice and generosity of
Stephen CuUnjieng. We are deeply grateful for his ongoing support.
   This book was also made possible by funding from the USC Dana and David Dornsife College of
Arts, Letters, and Sciences; the USC Department of American Studies and Ethnicity; and the Choi
Chang Soo Foundation.
   Additional support was provided by generous contributions from: Fuad Ahmad, Tanzila Ahmed,
Kamil Ahsan, Jasmine Ako, Hari Alluri, Stine An, Akhila Ananth, Tiffany Babb, Manibha Banerjee,
Terry Bequette, Roddy Bogawa, Paul Bonnell, Thi Bui, Hung Bui, Cari Campbell, Nate Cavalieri, Susan
Chan, Sonali Chanchani, Jade Chang, Wah-Ming Chang, Alexander Chee, Anita Chen, Anelise Chen,
Jean Chen, Lisa Chen, Leland Cheuk, Floyd Cheung, Amy Chin, Elaine Cho, Jayne Choi, Judy Choi,
Jennifer Chou, Seo-Young Chu, Elizabeth Clements, Tuyet Cong Ton Nu, Timothy Daley, Matthew
Dalto, Lawrence-Minh Bùi Davis, Susannah Donahue, Daniel Dyer, Irving Eng, Fan Fan, Matthew
Fargo, Peter Feng, Sia Figiel, Sesshu Foster, Christopher Fox, Sylvana Freyberg, Naomi Fukuchi, Kelsey
Grashoff, Anthony Hale, KA Hashimoto, Jean Ho, Skye Hodges, Ann Holler, Huy Hong, Abeer Hoque,
Jonathan Hugo, Jimmy Hwang, Ashaki Jackson, Theresa Kang, Mia Kang, Lisa Kang, Andrew Kebo,
Vandana Khanna, Bizhan Khodabandeh, Swati Khurana, Ian Kim, Helen Kim Lee, Gwendolyn Knight,
Sabrina Ko, Robin Koda, Karen Koh, Juliana Koo, Sun Hee Koo, Eileen Kurahashi, Paul Lai, Jenny Lam,
Iris Law, Samantha Le, Catherine Lee, Hyunjung Lee, Whakyung Lee in memory of Sonya Choi Lee,
Winona Leon, Claire Light, Janine Lim, Edward Lin, Jennifer Liou, Carleen Liu, Mimi Lok, Pauline
Lu, Abir Majumdar, Jason McCall, Sally McWilliams, Rajiv Mohabir, Faisal Mohyuddin, Russell Morse,
Samhita Mukhopadhyay, Adam Muto, Wendy Lou Nakao, Jean Young Naylor, Dominique Nguyen,
Kathy Nguyen, Kim Nguyen, Vinh Nguyen, Viet Thanh Nguyen, Minkyung & Yun Oh, Tiffany Ong,
Eric Ong, Camille Patrao, Perlita Payne, Thuy Phan, Cheryline Prestolino, James Pumarada, Zhiyao
Qiu, Jhani Randhawa, Amarnath Ravva, Sam Robertson, Brendan Ryan, Jonathan Sands, Chaitali Sen,
Prageeta Sharma, Andrew Shih, Roch Smith, Luisa Smith, Nancy Starbuck, Rachana Sukhadia, Robin
Suhkhadia, Rajen Sukhadia, Kelly Sutherland, Willie Tan, Zhen Teng, Isabella Tilley, Wendy Tokuda,
Frederick Tran, Monique Truong, Kosiso Ugwueze, Patricia Wakida, Kelli Washington, Aviva Weiner,
Heather Werber, Rachel Will, Duncan Ryuken Williams, William Wong, Andrea Wu, Anita Wu & James
Spicer, Amelia Wu & Sachin Adarkar, Ann Yamamoto, Jihfang Yang, Max Yeh, Stan Yogi, Shinae Yoon,
Mikoto Yoshida, and many others.
   Additional support for Kaya Press is provided by the National Endowment for the Arts; the
Los Angeles County Board of Supervisors through the Los Angeles County Arts Commission; the
Community of Literary Magazines and Presses and the Literary Arts Emergency Fund; and the City of
Los Angeles Department of Cultural Affairs.

The GIRL BEFORE HER

by Line Papin

Translated from the French by
Adriana Hunter
& Ly Lan Dill

Ink&Blood

CONTENTS

Peace

In Việt Nam, there are places where people bury their loved ones for a period of three years in caskets appropriate to their size. Then, once that period has elapsed and the flesh has dissipated, whatever is left is transferred to a smaller box. Cemeteries are thus made up of small boxes of bones.

The first casket is a transient, public thing, a temporary resting place for bodies in motion, used to house a different body every three years. Its only purpose is to sift out bones. The second, smaller box, is permanent and entirely one's own. It contains nothing but bones. It's as if the flesh, changeable as it has been throughout life—sometimes fresh, plump, and smooth; sometimes wrinkled, sickly, and blemished; sometimes soft and dense; sometimes rough or sagging; sometimes scarred—no longer mattered. Once our flesh disappears, taking with it our earthly sentiments and our muddy emotions, all that's left are bones. Those essential things we feel in our bones.

Ultimately, all of us end up like this. And there's a certain comfort to it. It's comforting because it's so mundane. Whatever injustices, upheavals, and dangers we might have suffered in life; whatever joys, laughs, fears, loves, hatreds, resentments, passions...; whatever accidents, journeys, crises, or illnesses... No matter how life has bent and twisted each of us, our bones remain. Our human bones. What we were and what we had tried our utmost to become. It's only now that I understand just how deeply we must love, how sincerely we must forgive: all the way down to those final bones.

I'm at the airport, as I have been many times since my birth, caught between two continents, my right foot in one, my left in the other. As I wait for my flight, I wonder about all these planes constantly circling this spherical planet and all the people they leave behind. During our too-brief lives, we know and can talk about so much of what happens on the surface of this compact globe with its countries and seas. Yet we are somehow unable to stop the wars that keep erupting inside us.

On this particular morning, I'm sitting in an armchair, passport in hand, waiting. Everyone around me is holding this same document. Inside each, an identity has been recorded. It's quiet here. Everyone is leafing through magazines or typing away on their phones, minding their own business instead of judging one another as they might on the street or at a café. All of us are either leaving or arriving. Suspended between the earth and the sky, we clutch our scraps of identity, fearful of being rejected: *Where's your boarding pass, please go through security.* A buzzer sounds. *Remove your shoes, okay, you can go now...* How much more of this crap do I have to deal with? *Priority Boarding? Are you traveling economy or business class? Do you have a biometric passport?* We're all stripped naked here—human beings, nothing more. Some panic, others are relaxed, still others are impatient or nodding off or cutting in line... But all of us here are governed by the authority of planes, by buzzers that tell us to fasten our seatbelts just as we've taken them off. We wait.

The P.A. system makes an announcement: it's time to board.

Where am I going? To Việt Nam. To Hà Nội. Like I did five years ago, ten years ago, fifteen years ago. Like I do every time—always differently, always alone, trying to reconcile the past and the present, the two continents and my aching bones, my past selves and who I am today. Deep in my pocket is a pewter tag, a vestige of a time I don't remember. This irregularly shaped piece of metal, pierced and threaded through with a string that was once tied around my wrist, is confirmation of a birth. It's a rubber stamp on my heart, a proof of identity more powerful than a passport. Engraved on it is the number "396" — my birth number. On December 30th, 1995, I became the 396th baby delivered in that shabby Vietnamese hospital.

Whose baby am I? No one's. Or rather I'm the baby of every solitary journey I've made in search of an answer to this question.

Today, I'm coming in peace to close this chapter of this story.

Miss Papin? Please hurry, you're the last passenger! The plane's about to take off. The steward trots ahead of me, gesturing for me to board. I come running. There, we're all in our seats now, belted safely up. I can already hear Vietnamese being spoken: flight attendants, passengers, recorded voices. I've forgotten this language, but the melody of its tonal variations still feels familiar. I'm torn—do I want to listen or should I try to shut it out? The plane takes off. A round ball slowly spins on our screens. Around it curves a dotted line that shows the trajectory of a small, white plane. As the route unspools, these dots lengthen into dashes that wrap around the planet. I've watched images like this since I was a child. Even back then, I understood that you can't stop the Earth from spinning. But what about everyone we left behind? How long were we leaving them for? What will they do in the meantime? Where were we going, anyway? And what happens to our hearts? Where does our love for them fit within the dotted line?

On the screen, the dots concertina toward a city whose name is hidden now by the icon of a plane touching down. I'm here then. Hà Nội. The air outside is humid. An airport taxi opens its doors, and soon I'm heading towards the city. Palm trees flit by, motorbikes honk, colors blur... I've grown so much older and put myself through so much, yet here Hà Nội is, still here, still mine. I love her so much. Sitting in the taxi, I'm listening to the blare of traffic when suddenly my eyes tear up. I'm that little girl again, throwing herself into her mother's arms, the dust against her cheek, her face buried in her mother's smell. I love my country, damn it.

I see the faces of all the girls I have been—the three-year-old, the seven-year-old, the ten-year-old, the fifteen-year-old—all huddled together, all so different. We're sitting there together in the back of that taxi. I kiss each of them to let them know: *It's going to be fine. You'll see. This is why we came back, to make the pain go away. We've come to this country where it all started to try to understand what happened and why.* All at once, I drop my touristy English and start talking to the driver in Vietnamese, drawing out this now-foreign language from my mouth to talk of things this guy couldn't care less about: *I was born here, this is my country, too, my history is here, I have a right to be here even though I've been away for such a long time, even though I've lost the language and the codes, the friends and family I once had here. This country was once my mother, too.* The driver gives a noncommittal shrug; he thinks I'm crazy.

We've finally reached my destination. Now that I've come back— now that I'm at peace with myself—I can at last write this next chapter of a story that has seen so many births and deaths, such joy and pain, so many different wars. It is my story to tell after all.

First war

1945

Our story begins in a hollowed-out, little runt of a village that's no different from any of its neighbors. More like an oasis than a war zone, it sits thirty kilometers from Hà Nội and is filled with palm trees, bamboo groves, and green, edible plants. Colorful fruits punctuate the explosion of green: dusty gold grapefruits, red-orange mangoes, brick and ochre litchis, magenta dragon fruit...

The inhabitants of this village work the soil from dawn to dusk. They hunch over this land upon which they depend, gathering vegetables, picking fruit, herding buffaloes, harvesting rice... Both their toil and reward can be found beneath their feet. Though the earth is generous, every yield is a victory. Happiness exists in this place where villagers live alongside their lovingly tended crops, everyone subject to the same sky and sun, the same monsoons and droughts. Their families, their animals, and their hopes are all united here, children of the same mother.

Ripe grains of rice peek out from under tufts of jade. The odd fish ripples down the river. Nothing about this landscape is refined or tidy. Even the simple act of walking requires imposing one's will on the abundant vegetation, whether by pushing aside the tall grass to clear a path or stepping over fallen branches and puddles. And within all that green are the insects—ants and spiders and especially the mosquitoes, which always seem to collect around the buffalo stalls and chicken coops. They are especially drawn to the lake and the small pagoda hazy with burning incense that floats in the middle of it. Hiding under lotus flowers, they wait for the faithful dressed in their best robes to cross the bridge to their place of prayer before flitting out and biting them.

During the momentary periods of respite between the two annual harvests, this pagoda is where neighbors meet and generations mingle, parents bringing their children, the grandparents either following or leading the way. Villagers come to gaze out over the lotus flowers or light incense and offer prayers to the dead who lie ten meters away in the village cemetery. The buzz of insects is punctuated by laughter, conversation, chanting, and, at irregular intervals, the penetrating sound of a gong. It's a place to gather; a place where the living talk to the dead.

Across the lake, the village cemetery sways above the rice fields, its caskets of bones suspended between the clouds and their reflection in the water. The sun glints off tears of sorrow or joy as women wearing cone-shaped hats stoop calf-deep in water, their hands plunged into tufts of green to gather their meager harvests, their ancestors peacefully at rest beside them. Buffaloes strain against their yokes. Work and leisure stand shoulder to shoulder, animals helping humans, the sun beating down on the water. The wind blows across this landscape in which emerald is married to cyan. Each moment is held suspended in a perfect balance. Hidden away in the background of all this is the village itself, laid out haphazardly on irregular patches of land. The small, hand-built homes appear on the verge of collapse, yet they somehow manage to keep smiling as they prop each other up thanks to a limewashed breezeway or a buffalo stall or a small, precarious bridge. It's as if they're holding hands, their fingers touching through the verdant foliage. The dirt path that serves as a road is where all the action takes place. Farmers pass from one field to the next; women transport produce in baskets that hang from either side of their bicycles.

Here in this region, war means hunger. Japanese forces, whose occupation of Việt Nam began before WWII, lash out in the aftermath of the Allied invasion of Okinawa, destroying French Indochina's colonial administration and decimating Việt Nam's rice fields.

Whistling bullets announce that war has arrived in the village. On this bridge that regulates the flow of people in and out of the village, it appears in the form of three French soldiers covered in blood. They've been shot. Staggering, they drag themselves to the pagoda at the center of the lotus lake. Blood spills over the collars of their uniforms and onto the bridge. They appear to be dying. Villagers come running, horrified. Should they help? Who are these white men? One man pushes the others aside. *Excuse me, let me through.* The village leader is almost six feet tall and stands with his head held high. Leaning over the wounded men, he evaluates how badly they're injured, then signals for them to be carried to his home as quickly as possible. Their wounds are stitched up with whatever is available and treated with cloth bandages dipped in salt water.

1946

The village leader has two wives and six children. The wives get along well: one looks after all the children while the other goes to the market to sell fruits and vegetables. One devotes herself to housekeeping and dishwashing, the other to harvests and sales.

This amicable state of harmony is maintained until one morning in 1946. By this point, the revolution has already taken place: Hồ Chí Minh is president and the Japanese have been kicked out. Attention is now turning to the French and a new war that will last eight years. That morning, the second wife heads off to the market with her produce. She pedals across the bridge on a bicycle heavy with mangoes, bananas, herbs, chickens, and eggs. A gunfight breaks out. Finding herself trapped between the villagers behind her and the soldiers up ahead, she isn't able to back away quickly enough... A stray bullet takes her life. She doesn't make it back from the market that morning. She never comes home again. Instead, the first wife is left to cope with everything by herself: the harvests, the housework, the cooking, going to the market, and raising all six children.

1961

One of the village leader's children, a boy named Trang, decided at twenty that he wanted to teach the children from the village where he grew up, giving them lessons on authors and dates, words and facts. The benches in his classroom only ever saw a handful of students, but those who did come applied themselves, their heads bent over their books.

After U.S. soldiers arrived in 1961 to aid South Việt Nam's rebellion against Hồ Chí Minh, many young men from the village, including Trang's own brother, went off to join the army. Trang was now 23, but because he was a teacher, he was not required to enlist. Instead, he kept watch over his students on their school benches, his refuge from the war a two-sided roof made of literature and history.

One student who came to class day after day was particularly hardworking and passionate. She loved history, Napoleon in particular, and would write down every last detail of "Na Bô Lê Ông's" exploits, his name appearing on each line of her exercise book in handwriting that marched across the pages like tiny black ants. She came back to school again and again, hoping to hear the next installment of Napoleon's adventures, but she enjoyed the lessons about literature, too. She wanted to learn to read better, to hear about more authors. At sixteen, she was a rare beauty. But who was this young woman? Let's call her Bà.

Born in the same village as Trang—in fact only a few meters away from where he was still living—Bà lived in a household that also included two wives, as was customary in Việt Nam at the time. But the living arrangements there were not nearly as harmonious as they had been in Trang's. Bà's father was violent. He beat his two wives, who in turn fought with one another. One decided to flee the brutal blows and vicious words. Gathering up her courage, her pride, her bruises, her belongings, and her daughters, she ran away to live on her own. The village was small so she didn't get very far, but that didn't matter. She found herself a scrap of land, built herself and her children a sturdy little home made of clay, and went out to earn a living using her own two hands. Vũ Thị Gạo may once have been beaten, she may have been alone, but she was strong. And now she was raising two daughters on her own. She was Bà's mother.

Bà grew up never seeing her father and half-brother and, like any wounded child, she developed a natural resentment toward them. But now, at least, she could live as she pleased with her mother and sister. Like other girls in the village, Bà helped her mother in the fields and the garden. This pretty girl, with her thick black hair and pink cheeks spent her days stooped over her work, her hands scratched, her ankles deep in muddy water. Though Bà was profoundly gentle, her sharp intellect was wed to an integrity and sense of injustice that would later be colored by an unwavering determination—a combination that could at times be mistaken for anger.

But in 1961, when Bà was still just sixteen, she had no anger, only curiosity. She wanted to read, to learn things she'd never be able to in the fields. That's why she'd signed up for classes in the village. Trang's lessons enthralled her. It came as no surprise when, a few years later,

Trang and Bà got married. They had a daughter, then another, then a third.

By 1968, Trang was living in Hà Nội, where he'd gotten a job at a university. The war with the French had finished by then, but the war with the Americans was still raging on; bombs had now replaced the gunfire and bullets in the village.

Several times a month, Trang would pedal for hours on end in order to see his wife and three daughters. The rest of the time, his mother-in-law, his wife, and the three little girls lived together in the village without him.

Second war

Sisters

In a little village not far from Hà Nội live three sisters whose names all begin with the letter H. Like the Three Helens or the Three Graces, they each have their own unique qualities, their own personalities, their own special gifts. The first is tempestuous and rebellious with wavy hair and a determined expression. She's fearless. The second is reserved, diligent, and sharp-eyed behind a silky curtain of straight hair. She's perceptive. The third has tightly curled hair and is gentle, delicate, and easy going. She knows how to enjoy herself.

All three are born amidst the sound of bombings; their country is buckling under the weight of seven million tons of explosives dropped by American planes. All three are beautiful but scrawny. All three are strong. They were born this way; they didn't have any other choice. They are Bà's daughters.

Like children everywhere, their world is filled with laughter, friends, games of hide and seek. But it's also scarred by thunderous explosions and suffering, by ration tickets and empty stomachs. From 1968 to 1975, anti-war protests erupt around the world, their impact rippling all the way to the White House; Văn Tiến Dũng replaces General Giáp; and two thousand civilians are killed in the Christmas Bombings. This is life as they know it. They live in their grandmother's home, three generations living under the same roof. Bà looks after her mother and her three daughters. Money is scarce. They own a pig they're fond of but will end up eating without regret because everyone's too hungry. The only treasures the girls own are candy wrappers they collect and trade with other children in the village: a blue one for a red one, a green one for a yellow one... If they're lucky, they might even come across a silver wrapper that's fallen from the pocket of a Soviet soldier, which can be swapped for ten Vietnamese ones. They squabble over these crumpled pieces of paper that are their most prized possessions and their only currency.

The bombs are deafening. No one knows how many more there will be, how long the war will last. The village bridge once crossed by three blood-soaked French soldiers has become the only viable route for the transfer of men and supplies from the North all the way down to Sài Gòn in the South. It shudders all day long under the rumble of trucks and tanks. If the Americans succeed in destroying this bridge, Hồ Chí Minh's soldiers will be stranded and cut off from their supply lines, so it's attacked regularly. But every time it's bombed, the villagers rush to patch it up; whatever happens, they won't let their beloved bridge be destroyed. Their desperate, human, almost elegant attempt to rebuild it are the only reason it's still standing. The result is a series of eccentric reinforcements—concrete supports that buttress the bridge every two meters. With its feet set in concrete and its ungodly number of crutches, the bridge looks like an old lady who's been put back together after a fall and can no longer stand straight.

To protect her granddaughters from the constant bombings, Vũ Thị Gạo sets up a little lean-to behind the house. With their father in Hà Nội and their mother and grandmother working in the fields, the three sisters—all still under the age of six—are left to their own devices. They play at home like puppies. When a bomb shatters the sky, they do as they've been told and run to the shelter and hide. Crouched in the dark, they huddle together and wait. How long? They don't know. Can they come out now? They don't know. Is this what it's like to die? They don't know. This is their childhood. This is Việt Nam in the early 1970s.

I've found two black and white photos from this period. The first is of the three H sisters and their mother. They're sitting in front of a house with a barred window. The youngest is on Bà's lap; the other two are pressed up against her, one to her right and one to her left. Together, the four of them form a single creature with eight skinny legs and eight skinny arms. All they have is one another. This is clear enough from the rough walls of their tiny home, the faded clothes they wear, and their bare feet, but it's also evident in the expression on the second H's face. *What's going to happen to us?* she seems to be wondering. *How will we cope?*

The second black and white photo is more cheerful. In it, Bà stands on a heap of straw or wood with the third H in her arms. There's a grove of bamboo behind them. Both mother and child are beaming.

Very little remains from that period: just these two photographs and a handful of stories about how, for example, the impetuous eldest sister once asked their mother for a few coins because she wanted to meet up with friends and had been angrily refused. If the eldest daughter were somehow to get pregnant on one of these evening excursions, no one would want anything to do with her. In the village, girls were still often compared to ticking time bombs, capable of dropping another mouth to feed into a household without warning. For something like that to happen in their household would be unthinkable. The first H howled in protest while the younger two stifled their laughter. That night, once everyone was in bed, the first H got up in the dark and fumbled for her clothes, throwing them on haphazardly. The other two watched her shadow move across the wall as she stole money from her mother's secret box and slipped out on tiptoe.

Perhaps it was the war that filled Bà with so much anger, that made Bà afraid yet prevented her from acknowledging her fears. The girls had no idea why their mother was the way she was, all they knew was that she was always saying no: no to requests for money—she would never give them any, she never had any; no to outings with friends—she never wanted them to go out; no to keeping the pig; to keeping their hair long; to every simple pleasure. The three sisters stood together, united against both their mother and the war.

Their existence was horrifyingly tenuous. Just skin and bones themselves, all they had to eat were bones. Bones were what they cuddled in their arms, what they dreamt of. Bones under bombs. Bones in photographs.

Not satisfied with merely looking after her daughters and working in the rice fields, Bà also volunteered in the village school. In her one free hour, she taught literature to a handful of students, introducing them to writers and reading them poems and novels. Becoming a teacher also meant there was a chance she could join her husband in Hà Nội. Trang had already asked everyone he knew about possible primary school openings, but had yet to receive any replies.

Whenever he could, Trang would go visit his family in the village, bicycling for hours to get there. He never had a moment to himself. In Hà Nội, if he wasn't busy with his classes, he was dealing with the unrelenting war. One evening, as staff and students were heading home from the university, news of a bombing came in over the public address system. Thirty of the university's tallest, strongest men were needed to help transport the wounded. Trang answered the call, carrying the poor, bleeding, suffering casualties on his back or in his arms as he took them to the hospital or the morgue.

He was on his way to school one day when someone pulled him

aside to tell him there was a job for Bà in Hà Nội. Wanting to share the good news with his wife, he pedaled back to the village faster than ever before. But his arrival was greeted by four devastated faces. Vũ Thị Gạo had died.

There was no reason for Bà to stay in the village now that her mother had died, so she and Trang left. They said goodbye to the dirt road, to the paths strewn with branches, to the greenery and the pagoda and the rice fields. Their time in the village had come to an end. Hà Nội, that sprawling, buzzing city, beckoned, opening her arms wide to welcome the young couple and their three daughters. The war would soon be over.

I can't help but think about Bà and her mother and those three girls in the village. I think about how they lived together during the war, all five of them, on their own, under that one meager roof—about the things they must have said to one another, the bombs they must have endured, the grains of rice they must have shared, their bones and their bruises, but also their laughter. I think about their nails, their teeth, their eyes, their arms, their hearts. I think about their black hair.

Young women

The war was over but Việt Nam was still struggling. Its harvests had been scorched and unexploded bombs still littered the countryside. Meanwhile, the American embargo made trade with other countries impossible. People had nothing: no electricity, no drinking water, no soap or toothpaste or shoes, no fridges or kitchen utensils. Nothing. But they barely even noticed their own poverty. Things had always been like this; there was nothing else to compare it to. Vietnamese newspapers remained upbeat, trumpeting news about the country's invincibility and how the rest of the world was terrified of its progress. The country was thriving and everything was wonderful! What a triumph! So what if no one had scooters or cars, so what if people were starving to death? It was the same everywhere. *Look at these photos of the French clutching tickets while standing in line. They're even hungrier than we are!* What the newspapers didn't say was that these crowds weren't waiting for food, they were lined up in front of a movie theater. Photos of people outside concert halls were cropped to show that everyone all over the world was starving too. All of which was reassuring.

Newly arrived in the capital, Bà and Trang set up home in a small apartment on the fourth floor of a simple building. The girls all slept in the same bed in a room that looked out over a noisy road. Bars covered the windows. Through it, the acrid sweat and heat of burnt-out Hà Nội would rise into their apartment, along with the smell of scorched grass, the thrum and honking of motorbikes, the calls of vendors desperately hawking their handful of mangoes, the wails of children, the cadence of manual laborers, barking dogs, clucking hens... The chaos, in sum, of a crowd intent on surviving no matter what. Bà closed the windows. She didn't want the girls to cough.

The sisters never had a chance to be just teenagers. All they ever knew was work: work at school and work at home. They cooked and cleaned in that concrete apartment that was so unlike their former home in the village. They unwound skeins of wool to sell to factories, earning what they could to help their parents. They went to fetch water from the well, washed without soap, brushed their dark hair with grapefruit juice and their teeth with salt. They lacked pretty clothes and proper shoes; they were thin and dirty. But they were beautiful. And now they were grown.

As they grew accustomed to the capital, they came to love it as much as the teeming crowds who shouted themselves hoarse in their struggle to survive. In the mornings, the three Hs biked or walked to school or to the factory. They locked arms with one another and with those around them. It was the 1980s. Sparks from construction sites drifted across streets rife with poverty, noise, and people; the occasional smell of cooking mingled with coal smoke. The city was recovering from the disasters of war; its inhabitants claimed victory even as they wept in pain. It was because they were poor—but also because they had won— that they loved one another.

Having inherited a love for literature and history from Trang and Bà, the girls took their schoolwork seriously. The second H was selected for a study year abroad, but the only exchange programs available were in other communist countries: Poland, Russia, or East Germany. So Moscow it was. Before flying out, the second H was told the flip-flops she usually wore were utterly inappropriate for Russia, something she'd realize as soon as she landed. So, gathering all her savings, she went to the market to find more suitable footwear. She searched for three consecutive days before finally finding a stall that sold sandals with proper soles. It was in these new sandals that she stepped out for the first time onto Moscow's snowy sidewalks.

When the second H returned home after a year in Russia, she came back with candy whose wrappers would have been worth a fortune in their childhood currency. She also brought back museum-worthy snow boots, the likes of which had never been seen before in Hà Nội, as well as heavy, cast-iron cooking pans she planned to sell. Cast-iron pans were rare in Việt Nam; only the wealthiest families could afford them. But the Vietnamese versions were so thin as to be pretty much useless. Sometimes they would even catch fire along with the vegetables being cooked inside them. By melting one of the Russian pans down to make ten Vietnamese ones, everyone was able to turn a profit, paltry as it was.

The sisters grew into women in a Việt Nam impoverished by the embargo. Though they were poor, they weren't unhappy: they still lived under the same roof with their parents, and they were united, hardworking, and quick to laugh. And their story would have a happy ending: they would turn twenty, meet men, have children... Yes, they would live happily ever after. Together.

They still looked like girls as they walked side by side, tall and beautiful, their jet-black hair flowing down their backs. And yet they had become three mothers with children in their arms.

Their story goes something like this: the first H got married and had two sons; an architect asked for the hand of the third; and the second, the middle sister, met a French man in a camera shop while visiting a friend who worked there. This young tourist had fallen under the spell of this former enemy country. Having taken an inordinate amount of photos, he was bringing them to the shop to get developed just as the second H was leaving. The result was what is often called love at first sight. He started wooing her on the spot. Despite her friend's head-shaking and arm-waving just behind the young man—*He's French! He's a sweet-talker! He's dangerous!*—the second H was charmed. She was not as spirited as her elder sister or as easy-going as the youngest, rather, she was inquisitive and observant. Which is why she didn't wave the French man off or cross her arms until he went away. She was the middle sister, the one whose arms were always reaching out for opportunities. And so she continued to see him discreetly.

They were a good match, so much so that their relationship quickly became vital to both of them. The second H braved the misgivings of her friends, her sisters, and her parents, and continued to spend time with the French man. Bà and Trang were strongly opposed to the possibility of their most sensible daughter marrying the enemy. This fling of hers was absurd, an act of terrorism, a political stand against her country, couldn't she see that? The war was still tearing apart both flags, one blue, white, and red and the other red with a yellow star. But the lovebirds couldn't have cared less. They communicated in English, waiting for the French man's Vietnamese lessons to produce results. They gazed into each other's eyes. He peered out at her through glasses perched on the end of a long, thin nose and she peeped out from under the bangs of black hair that skimmed the top of hers. It was the first time either of them had fallen in love.

She invited him home to meet her two sisters and their husbands as well as her parents, who disapproved of the match. The French man ate with the family in the main room. Everyone sat in a circle on the floor around a tablecloth and used chopsticks to take food from the dishes that had been set out on it. The children ran around the adults as they ate and occasionally leaned against their backs... At first, the French man's presence cast a wary pall over everyone—especially Bà, who was particularly upset with her daughter's choice. Having lived through the first war with the French, she couldn't understand how a child of hers could have turned towards the enemy, towards a life different from the classic Vietnamese one, with its values and traditions. How could the second H turn away from the family's history of resistance? Why did she have to pick a foreigner and, to make things worse, a French man? Why run away to a different country with different customs and a different grammar?

But the French man proved to be a good guy. He, too, was interested in history and literature and he was making considerable progress in his efforts to learn Vietnamese. So, gradually, the family learned to like him, and to relax and enjoy themselves even when he was around. They even began to accept him as one of their own. He came to the house regularly now, riding his Minsk, a thirty-year-old Russian motorbike that was tricky to start up and would break down every couple of meters, spewing out as much smoke as a truck. He often brought with him chocolate or some other Western treat that he'd managed to procure from the diplomatic containers that were delivered every three months to the French embassy. Drawing up a list of items requested by the family, the young man would collect whatever was needed from the back of a truck to share with them.

This young student of history, who had successfully passed the notoriously rigorous and prestigious upper-level French teaching exams, eventually gained the family's trust. Bà began asking him to clarify a few details about Napoleon's adventures for her. She would take notes, comparing what he said to what she knew. Meanwhile, the French man was himself becoming increasingly fond of the family and its ways.

When, after a year of courtship, the French man suggested that the second H meet his parents in France, the Vietnamese family became suspicious all over again. What if he abducted her? What if he killed her? What if he sold her? In post-war Việt Nam, an actual love story involving a French man and a Vietnamese woman was still too much of a fairy tale. The only solution for a problem like this was for them to get married. So that's what the family told him.

The French man was young and determined. And so, a year after they first met, he and the second H were married in a traditional Vietnamese ceremony complete with a special red áo dài. The bride's face was painted so white that her husband-to-be didn't even recognize her when she joined him.

And that was that. Their marriage marked the end of the war, the end of childhood, the end of the three sisters' non-existent adolescence. They were three grown women now, three wives, three mothers with three husbands, all living under the same roof as Bà, who still kept a watchful eye over everyone and everything.

Bà was now forty-five. She had married off her daughters, her husband gave lectures at the university every week, and she herself was now a teacher... She had stayed the course and fulfilled her dreams. Her battles had borne fruit.

Mothers

The bellies of the two eldest Hs grew at the same time, forming maternal bumps on bodies still thin from having lived off of nothing but rationed rice. They were not yet twenty-five, and soon they would be mothers. Their bellies swollen, they stood next to each other in their childhood bedroom watching the busy road teeming with crowds thirsty for life through the window. The babies in their wombs would become familiar with, not rice fields, but rather motorbike horns; not ration tickets, but the smell of bún chả. Out in the main room, Bà was knitting two little outfits. She was going to be a grandmother. They'd managed to survive it all. Life would go on.

The next generation began with a pair of boys born on opposite sides of the world. The eldest sister's baby arrived in Việt Nam, while the second sister's son—half Vietnamese and half French, half yellow on red and half blue and white and red—was born in France. The French man, who found Vietnamese hospitals alarmingly rudimentary, wanted his wife to go to a clinic in France and had arranged for a last-minute flight. They ended up spending a few weeks there. The second sister slept for the first time ever on a soft mattress that made her so queasy, she threw up. She also ate pizza for the first time; it made her throw up. Then there was her morning sickness and the pregnancy itself... She was sick throughout her entire stay. But she loved France nonetheless.

After their son was born, they returned to her family and the cramped apartment in Hà Nội. Luckily it was now 1994, and the embargo had just been lifted. A tide of foreign products suddenly flooded the country. Shopkeepers had been preparing for this glut of commodities. In Hà Nội you could now buy Coca-Cola, toothpaste, soap, shampoo, chocolates, medicine, milk, and even diapers. Thank goodness it didn't take long for these items to reach Việt Nam, which meant the young father didn't have to bring any of it back from France himself.

Hà Nội's roads, which had until then been the almost exclusive domain of crisscrossing bicycles and cyclos, now saw the occasional Honda or Toyota scooter... Overhead, hundreds of black cables were being unspooled, bringing electricity to the city. They hung from wooden posts, a crackling, electric sky of wires constantly on the verge of catching fire, threatening disaster. But at least it was finally possible to plug in a few refrigerators and air conditioning units. Everything was unstable, unreliable, and dangerous. And all of it was new.

The third generation arrived at the same time as the foreign goods. They were turn-of-the-century, post-embargo children, they would know toothpaste and soap, and they reveled in this new prosperity, giddy with happiness.

A few months passed—months filled with new babies and evening meals eaten in a circle on the floor, with mothers, the grandmother, husbands, the grandfather, smells, voices, motorbikes. Hà Nội, once so disfigured, was beginning to look like a city again.

Then the accident happened.

Daughters

When you haven't yet thought things through for yourself but you suddenly create a being burdened with a life of its own, you have no choice but to take responsibility for it, for this accident; it's yours to carry, and you must do so without ever laying it down, from its start in an amniotic sea to its final casket of hard bones. *We never meant for this to happen; I wasn't thinking, I can't back out now, it's happening, that's life.* A few months after the second sister's return to Hà Nội, her belly started to swell again. She was already a young mother and her body, which had just barely regained its original form, was being distorted once more. She was carrying a new, unexpected life. And there were already too many people in the apartment.

Hà Nội's hospitals at the time were just buildings, places where women gave birth, not proper clinics. The doctors wore white coats but had few instruments. When the second sister arrived to leave her urine sample, the nurse aides were slaughtering a pig for the upcoming Tết holiday under the raw, wooden plank that was their makeshift counter. *Yes, leave that there!* someone said, pointing helpfully overhead with one hand while cutting into the pig with the other. Pregnant women set down their piss pots—Evian bottles, plastic jars, china cups, cooking pots, watering cans, even buckets—then left, navigating their way through the hospital's decrepit hallways and back out to the street. They'd been told to come back the following week. In the meantime, they could only hope that their results wouldn't get mixed up or lost.

The second H dropped off her bottle of urine as well. There it was, placed alongside the others, one translucent bottle among so many others. She'd decided to risk a pregnancy instead of attempting an abortion. Just then, she heard a crunch of bones from under the table. Blood sprayed up, leaving a scarlet stain on her pale clothes. The pig was dead.

We are born in specific places for specific reasons. We arrive brand new, carrying the bones of what came before—the bones of wars, the bones of the grandmother who had battled her way through them, the bones left behind by bombs, the bones of how quickly life changes, of three girls, three sisters, of all the no's they heard from their mother, of Hà Nội, of the first-born son, of all the things they ever considered or wondered about. And then there are the bones that are carried unknowingly, bones that might not have been wanted but exist nonetheless. Bones that will tear everything apart. And so, on December 30th, at the tail end of 1995, a little girl is born in that squalid hospital in the barely rebuilt city of Hà Nội. She arrives, thrilled to have snuck into existence, to have exploded into this lineage of women. Her story has no airplane or French clinic—instead, she is born into the misery and beauty of her country.

After the grandmother, after the three sisters, after all these tales of love and war, there you are: born in that dingy hospital where rats the size of newborns prowl up and down the hallways at night. While the mothers rest, the fathers take turns keeping watch over babies who haven't even been bathed or dressed yet, attacking the starving vermin with brooms. There you are in your baby carriage, up above those dark, menacing shadows, still wrapped in a blood-stained towel. In the morning, your brother comes to visit. He's only a year and half and horrified by the "peasant" he finds covered in placenta and dried blood from the night before. So the first thing he says is "Nhà quê!"

Yes, a whole night has passed while you lay up above the rats, still covered in placenta and caked in dried blood. December 30th has turned into December 31st. We're in Hà Nội, with its influx of new motor scooters, electric wires, shouts, and noise. And tomorrow it will be 1996. It's the end of one year and the beginning of another; the end of an era and the beginning of another.

Hà Nội 1996 is filled with the sounds of Vietnamese being spoken, but also of your father speaking French and your mother speaking English. There are faces, so many faces surrounding you—your grandmother, your nanny, your aunts. There are plenty of other sounds, too. All this is the life we love, that you love. And you're also introduced to the sun from which—as always in Việt Nam—no one can hide; heavy with humidity, it explodes above all this chaos. There's no escaping the smells, either, they're overpowering, omnipresent: grilled meat, bún chả, herbs, coal, gas. You, a baby still caked in blood, are born into all of this. Why bother being washed when all this grime is glorious, when all these shouts and smells swaddle you as tightly as these torn, old sheets? There's love to be found in these sheets, in these exclamations and smells—the love of a city that's finally living without constraints and loves its daughters without inhibition.

This little girl filled with unbridled joy came hurtling into this life, into Hà Nội 1996, into a never-ending summer camp filled with kids, bicycles, cyclos, into constant comings and goings... This was our life. We ran around outdoors, free. The air was heavy on our skin, telling us, *I won't forget you, you're not alone. I'm here, pressed up against you. I'm life,*

Hà Nội, and I'll always be with you, always, holding you close. As long as you're with me, you'll be free and alive.

Hà Nội 2000, there's been nothing like it since. Newborn babies arrived along with an influx of foreign goods, and both were greeted with equal enthusiasm. They basked in this newfound peace, this new era. We loved each other here because the embargo had been lifted along with our hearts. Because that's what we had always done.

The little girl crawled around the family's circle on the floor, she saw the faces and the long black hair of the three sisters, she heard their voices. She was the first granddaughter. I can see her, this child who was me—her happy face, her laughter and dimples, her joy. I say hi to her and smile knowingly because although she doesn't know us yet, we know her, we know her future, what is going to happen to her. And we want to save her. I tell her to be careful, but also that everything's going to be okay. She's just a little girl, an accident who surprised everyone.

By being a girl, she surprised her grandmother most of all.

Bà had been raised during a war by a single mother; she barely knew her father. Then she'd lived through a second war, this time with three little girls of her own and never a moment to rest. But when her first granddaughter was born, Bà loved her. I can confirm this because the little girl felt it. I felt it. Bà loved this little girl in a way her own mother hadn't been able to, in a way she herself hadn't been able to, in a way her daughter wasn't able to. Freed from war and, as a grandmother, from the tight and complicated ties between mother and daughter, she claimed this little girl. And in so doing, she decided to claim the girl's birthday as well.

No birth certificate, nothing signed or official had ever existed that could confirm Bà's date of birth. Her own mother, who couldn't read or write, didn't know the year in which her daughter had been born, much less the month. When Bà needed to apply for a work ID, she had to do some digging: *Try to remember,* she pleaded, but her mother honestly didn't know. The best she could do was to say, *You were born at about the same time as that neighbor over there.* So Bà went off to inquire with the neighbor, which gave her an approximate idea of her birth month. Then she turned to her own memories: she recalled the feeling of sitting and being hungry at the same time, which meant she could already sit up in that year when everyone was starving. Yes, she remembered the famine of 1945, the one that struck North Việt Nam because the Japanese had replaced the rice fields needed to feed the population with jute fields that served only to make uniforms for their army. That year, many people died of hunger. She must have been a year old at the time. Did that mean she was born in 1944?

She probably used this same technique to get an ID card for her mother, my great-grandmother. When rummaging through an old closet one day, I came across it. Issued on September 11, 1978 to Vũ Thị Gạo, it lists her date of birth as January 10, 1920. On the back of the card are her fingerprints and a physical description: "Nốt ruồi nói cách 1 cm dưới trước đầu lông mày phải," which means: "A nascent mole appears roughly 1 cm below her right eyebrow." There's a photo glued to the front of the card. I turn it over to check the accuracy of this meticulous description and discover Vũ Thị Gạo's face. Both her ears stick out from under the traditional turban she's wearing, and her brows are knitted together into determined folds. Her mouth is turned down making her expression look defiant, as if to say, *Yeah, so what? You got a problem with me?* But her eyes communicate a gentleness that softens her stern expression. Her clearly defined chin is held high and juts forward from her thin neck. She is slender and proud with narrow shoulders, and everything about her is intimidating. I can't see any trace of the mole that purportedly "appears" one centimeter below her right eyebrow, but I can imagine it, or rather I can imagine the office worker who'd been assigned to my great-grandmother when she came for her ID card. I can picture him hesitating briefly as he leans closer to her, studying her face, then shrugging and scrawling, "mole appears 1 cm…" and validating the card with his red stamp before yelling, *Next!* My great-grandmother leaves, making way for the next applicant. Printed on the card in her pocket is her name: Vũ Thị Gạo. This makes me smile. Gạo means "grain of rice." To have the name *Grain-of-rice* in a time of famine must have been like being called *Happiness* or *Luck* or *Sunshine*.

When Bà's granddaughter was born, it was still possible to make changes to personal records. Other people had already been filing complaints, corrections, and retractions, so Bà decided to make a correction of her own; from here on out, she would write on any and all official papers that she'd been born on December 30th. She liked the baby's date of birth the way she liked the baby's face. After all the wars, after all the beatings and bruises and ration tickets, a baby had come unexpectedly into Bà's world. This girl with a life of her own, this tiny bomb intended not for bridges but rather for cuddling in your arms, had been born on the 30th of December. And now, so was Bà.

Granddaughters

People come at dawn to exercise in Công viên Lê Nin, the park that sits in the heart of Hà Nội. There they are for all to see, their arm movements expansive in the morning air. During the day, when everyone is at work, the park stands empty except for a few passing baby-strollers. In the evenings, it fills up again with children meeting up after school or athletic adults enjoying a game of badminton after a long day... Then when the sun goes down, the park closes and everyone goes home, leaving the greenery in solitude once more.

Bà used to go to Công viên Lê Nin three times a day. It wasn't far from her apartment building, so that's where she did her morning exercises and played badminton in the evenings. And, in the middle of the day, it's where she took her granddaughter for a walk, pushing her along proudly in an old stroller whose wheels would wobble and squeak as the child's wriggling caused the seat's fabric to rip. Bà was a formidable woman in her early fifties. Though no longer beautiful, she was still arresting, her features hardened by resolve. She wore black sunglasses, a silk scarf, and long, flowery dresses. Her curly, still-black hair framed a stern face. Nothing could faze her now; she'd come this far on her life's journey, and now here she was, taking her own birth date for a walk in a stroller.

Holding this innocent, chubby-cheeked baby girl must have felt a lot like hope for a woman like Bà. She had seen so many broken, worn-down women in her lifetime: her mother had fled an abusive husband, and though her daughters were married now, they used to have to shelter from bombs. But here was this new little baby girl upon whom Bà could shower more of her time and love than she had ever done with anyone else. She read the girl stories under the mosquito nets, turning over the pages with her long fingers. She played hide-and-seek with her and always lost, her pink plastic shoe always managing somehow to peep out from behind a bush. *Found you!* Whenever she was with her granddaughter, she would lean in close with every part of herself: her black hair, her arms, her skin and lips, her rasping voice, her unrelenting gaze. She was hard on everyone else, serving them a brew of anger and bitterness that she felt was justified because of all the effort she put into cooking, doing the housework, and going to the market. Bà had a lot on her shoulders, the child could sense this in her eyes and in her voice. Things weighed her down, and she sometimes made others pay for this. But never her granddaughter.

An essential triangle bound the two of them together. The child had been born on December 30th, and the number inscribed on the metal tag around her wrist at birth to distinguish her from all the other babies in the hospital had been three hundred ninety-six. So she'd come into the world surrounded by multiples of three. This became something she clung to and would later claim as her own. When other kids in the schoolyard would ask her what her favorite number was, she would always say, *Three.* Why? It was instinctual. Perhaps it had something to do with the number's rounded shape, which didn't have sharp edges, like 2 or 4, both of which looked spiky and dangerous. Unlike the number 1, the number 3 wasn't bland. The only good thing about the number 1 was its position, which had not been earned but rather granted, and thus could never be taken away. Deep down, the number 1 was a weakling. You come first, it was told, after which it stopped making any effort at all. As for the number 5, it didn't have a care in the world. Plump and little, it sat at the end of the line where nothing could harm it. But the number 3 was measured and reserved, neither too exposed nor too hidden, broad enough to be generous, yet restrained enough to be sincere. The little girl also identified with the number 3 because it was in the middle of numbers 1 through 5. Most importantly, perhaps, all that was required for "ba," the word for the number 3, to become "Bà", or grandmother, was a shift in tones. It was comforting to think of this silly series of connections as forming a triangle.

This amusing—or ridiculous—coincidence became for the little girl additional proof of the relationship between her and her grandmother, a connection that lasted right up until Bà's final hours. People always commented on it: *There's something special between the two of you*, they would say. *She's especially fond of you.* But this empathy and love, this bond that had skipped a generation, also meant that the little girl could feel the bruises from all the wars her grandmother carried within herself. Yes, this little girl carried those bruised hearts and bones within herself, too.

One day, the second H and her French husband decided to move out of the family apartment. The young man's upbringing hadn't prepared him to live with grandparents, aunts, and uncles. He wanted a place where his wife, son, and daughter could live on their own. This way of thinking offended the grandparents—and the grandmother in particular. Bà had always hoped to live under the same roof with her daughters, as she herself had done with her own mother. She was also strongly opposed to her little granddaughter sleeping on her own.

According to her, children should sleep in their parents' beds; that's how things were done in Việt Nam. But the French father thought babies should have bedrooms of their own. The very thought of this was disconcerting for Bà. *Without me, this little girl's mother would never have been born, and so she wouldn't have been born either.* She comes from me, so she needs to live with me, she insisted. But Bà had no say in the matter, and over her protests, the family moved to a new home at 501 Kim Mã Street. It was just down the road and dropping in to visit the grandparents was easy.

The family's new residence, an unexpectedly horizontal white slab, contrasted starkly with the other buildings in the neighborhood, which were all vertical and gray. Parking of any kind was forbidden at the complex, which meant there were no crowds of scooters, cyclos, and bicycles lined up in front of it, no stalls selling noodles and barbecued pork, no shoe-shine boys and pop-up hairdressers. Instead, its gate was monitored by four guards in sentry boxes; in order to gain access to this clean, calm, rarefied place, you needed either to live there or be granted special authorization to visit. Such exclusivity came at a price: only expatriates could afford the homes here. As a result, the residents were Canadian or Russian or English or Australian or Italian or French. The lingua franca at 501 Kim Mã Street was English, a language the children quickly learned so they could talk with one another. Like all the other children growing up at the complex, the second H's son and daughter came to associate English with privilege; Vietnamese was the language of the streets. Once a week, the two would shift between comfort and chaos as they made their way up the street to visit Trang and Bà, the noisy commotion of their grandparent's place a stark contrast to the gilded silence of the gleaming white complex, with its carousel and swimming pool.

These visits were rarely reciprocated; Bà was unsettled by the idea of having to go through a gate, pass by a watchman, and announce that she was a "guest." This was her city, her country, after all. Why should she, someone who'd built up a life for her family from nothing, refusing to be daunted by any challenge, now have to jump through hoops just to visit her own grandchildren? It was intolerable, as were the snooty looks she noticed, or perhaps imagined, once she passed through the housing compound's gates. Her long flowery dresses and plastic sandals were elegant outside 501 Kim Mã, but once inside, who could say? To avoid all this unpleasantness, Bà preferred to see her grandchildren in her own home.

This arrangement suited everyone. Bà and Trang no longer lived under the same roof as their grandchildren, whose father had inevitably passed on to them his own very different culture, but they eventually learned to adapt to this new half-Western way of life. The children, for their part, enjoyed the weekly ritual of walking to their grandparents' home. Along the way, they would often stop at a grocery store called L's Place that sold pink popsicles. These strawberry-flavored ice-pops—so insignificant and yet so much better than anything else—were really just colored water, but oh, what high aspirations they had. They were the very embodiment of a resolve to do better, to imitate the West, the wealthy. *Pink popsicles!* The children pounced on them excitedly. *Strawberry- and raspberry-flavored popsicles! How cool!* The children couldn't have cared less about the popsicles' ambitions or even how they tasted—they just knew they wanted them. How they squabbled over those pink ice pops! The little girl stole her brother's and licked it; he pulled her hair and they both laughed. The two looked almost like twins, with their identical black hair and similar builds, but the boy was already a bit more sensible, and the little girl had alsways been more playful.

For the little girl, walking into L's Place was always a special treat. It was just twenty square meters, but it felt like a luxury boutique, one filled with food, clothes, and all sorts of Western knickknacks such as colorful hair scrunchies, stickers, shampoo, sparkly hair combs, and stuffed animals. Everything came from America or Europe; everything was packaged and almost pristine. The child would strut up and down the aisles, trying on sequined headbands that cost thousands of đồngs. Whistling and singing to herself, she'd pick up a bit of cheap plastic as if it were a precious jewel... Then someone would insist, *We need to go, Line! Hurry up!* And with one last glance over her shoulder, she would reluctantly leave the store. Her grandmother was inevitably irritated whenever the child arrived with something from L's Place. She was the only little girl in the neighborhood with painted nails and barrettes and headbands. With her plastic treasures and her strawberry popsicles, she was quite the little princess.

At lunch time the extended family still ate as they always had, aunts and uncles, fathers and mothers, siblings and friends, old and young, all sitting together in a circle on the floor, plates of food laid out in the middle so they could help themselves to anything they liked. If you weren't deft enough with your chopsticks, you risked being left hungry. While the adults chatted, the kids would fight over the best pieces of meat. Then they would head off to play in the bedroom where Bà kept her incredible electrical exercise contraptions, or they would chase the cats that loved to hide among the dusty suitcases stowed beneath a bed with wooden slats. And the children's secret pleasure? Winding up a little wooden music box and listening to it play *Für Elise* their first lullaby. Then the visit would be over and the girl's family would leave and go home.

Nannies

Cô Phái, a young woman the same age as the second H, was the eldest of five children. Needing to find work, she offered her services as a nanny, housekeeper, and cook to the second H, who was exhausted and overwhelmed. The couple took a liking to Cô Phái and decided to hire her. Then the little girl was born. When the family moved to 501 Kim Mã Street, Cô Phái came with them. Her duties included taking care of the housework often, the cooking sometimes, and the little girl all the time. The other member of their household, a chauffeur named Chú Tú, was responsible for driving the family's Galloper—one of the only large cars in the city.

Cô Phái and Chú Tú both remained at 501 Kim Mã Street for many years as part of the family. The children would scurry around the Galloper and climb onto Chú Tú's knee, begging to be allowed to drive. He'd laugh, take one last drag on his cigarette and stub it out. *Sorry kids*, he'd say before climbing into the vehicle and roaring off. The sound of that big engine was unmistakable—the children could pick it out from miles away. The moped Cô Phái arrived on could only be heard once she was through the gate. It had been given to her by the young French man to make it easier for her to get to her parents' house on her days off. Accepting such a huge gift was difficult for Cô Phái—that Honda was worth a fortune at the time—but it meant she would no longer have to walk in the sun for kilometers on end without a hat or proper shoes.

Life was good. The young French man worked all day in his office at the French School of the Far East. He tracked down unpublished documents that allowed him to compile a historical study of Việt Nam, the likes of which had never been seen before. He was so enamored with this country, which had captivated him even in its raw, 1990s state, that not only did he decide to move there, he also: married the second H and, in the process, her whole family; worked hard to become fluent in Vietnamese; had Vietnamese children; and even went so far as to make Việt Nam the focus of his job and the subject of his research. The young student who'd once been interested in sixteenth-century France had transformed himself into a historian of Việt Nam,

During the day, neither parent was ever present in the house at 501 Kim Mã Street. The second H's innate curiosity and energy meant that she was always attending to a thousand and one different things, opening her arms wide to whatever life had to offer. She, too, traveled about on her own little Honda moped, which she used to visit her sisters and her mother. Now that she lived in a residential complex full of expatriates, and her husband was a tây whom people would point at because there were still so few foreigners in Hà Nội, her circumstances were more comfortable than ever before. Rationing, bombs, and makeshift shelters were no longer a part of her life. She dressed more elegantly than her sisters, sometimes even with the occasional accessory. A photo taken by Bà shows the three sisters sitting in a living room. The eldest, dressed in the same puffy, red nylon windbreaker that the third H wears in a different photo, is holding a piece of fruit and looking casually into the lens. Beside her, the gentle youngest H looks down at the flowers on the coffee table. She's wearing a blue and black sweatshirt that Bà wears in another photo. The second H is sitting slightly apart and to the left, her legs neatly aligned, her arms crossed, her back straight. With her earrings, pearl necklace, lipstick, silk blouse worn under a fine-knit sweater, and sky-blue linen pants, she's the most stylish person there, the most well turned-out. But on her face is the same anxious expression she wears as a child in that photograph of her in the village.

So few Vietnamese could travel back then; visiting France was as distant a dream as going to the moon. But she had been there. She had even given birth there. Her children were mixed-race, and she was no longer poor. Her life had changed so quickly, everything about it was different. Just take a look at her daughter, all decked out in plastic tiaras from L's Place.

During the day, 501 Kim Mã was more or less empty and Cô Phái could do as she pleased. She willingly took charge of the house and enjoyed watching the children grow. And she fell head over heels for the little girl—you know that because you were there. Cô Phái loved you from the moment you were born on December 30, 1995. She would hold you in her arms, and kiss and comfort you. She agreed to your every whim: to another square of French chocolate, to potatoes in your rice, to going out to play with your friends after dinner when it was already getting dark, to organizing dance recitals. She helped you print giant posters that you then stuck illegally on the walls of the complex. She always said yes to you: to outrageous make-up and nail polish and outlandish hairdos, to trips to L's Place and those famous fake-strawberry popsicles.

Cô Phái and the child were never apart. The nanny sometimes even slept on a mattress at the foot of the child's bed. People would often stop the little girl in the street, stroke her hair and pinch her cheeks, ask her where she was from and if she was Tây or Việt... And when the child would run to hide behind Cô Phái, she would cry *Mommy!*

Cô Phái's heart beat for that little girl — the child could feel it. The young woman was filled with maternal affection, her feelings were protective, visceral, intimate. She needed to love the little girl, she wanted to love her, and she did love her, holding her tightly in her arms. The attachment between them was apparent. What the child felt for Cô Phái was a daughter's love for her mother. Cô Phái held her in her arms—yes, held you, not your brother or anyone else. She held you tight, lifting you away from the bruises and bombs, from the dingy hospital filled with rats and bloodied sheets and a metal tag inscribed with the number 396. From the bones that came before.

The adults drifted in and out of 501 Kim Mã Street. One young woman coming home on her Honda would cross paths at the gate with another young woman who was on her way out; one young man arriving in the Galloper would see the other leaving... We were tiny boats pitching about in constant motion, like a runaway wave, like Hà Nội itself. No one worried about pre-assigned roles. The four adults did things in their own way and as they saw fit. We were living in a society that was based on Communism and community, but this was different. This had nothing to do with ideology and everything to do with love. You, a peasant who had come into this world smeared with placenta and blood, had been gathered up by your tenacious grandmother and tended to by your loving nanny with her worn-out flip flops. And now here you were, running around the air-conditioned rooms of a residential complex adorned in plastic rhinestones. You were surrounded by your father, your mother, your brother, and your friends, two or three of whom always seemed to be hanging out in the living room. Yes, love and support were all around you. Here in Việt Nam you had five families, five anchor points to which you could always return, whatever happened: your city, your parents, your nanny, your grandparents, and your friends. They enfolded you daily, creating a home within which your heart beat happily. You loved them when you woke up, and when you went to bed, you didn't leave them behind. Yes, you had five families, but you also had three mothers—the second H, your grandmother, and your nanny—and you swam happily between all of them. Nuclear families didn't make sense here. The street was our family, and you its free, itinerant, water baby.

Water constantly surrounded us, whether from a recent rain or at the complex's pool, where we could always be found splashing around. Even after we dried ourselves off, the humidity in the air would cling to us like a second skin from whose protective embrace it was impossible to emerge.

At 501 Kim Mã Street, children scampered about naked or in their underwear or swimsuits, they straddled the horses on the carousel, splashed in the pool, or simply flopped to the ground to chat. They played, swam, ran, bicycled: by bedtime, they had already packed three days' worth of activities into one. But they weren't tired: they wanted… What did they want? To keep going, to keep talking, playing, living. The children at 501 Kim Mã Street craved life. They thirsted for it. The sun, the heat, friends, their families, the constant noise—what else could they possibly need? Drink, drink, drink it all in. They were ardent and insatiable for the world around them. During the monsoon, the lake would flood, flowing right into the gardens until the little children were chin-deep in water. To get from one place to the next, they would row boats, fishing rod in hand, and catch muddy gray fish that they found beautiful simply because they were fish. And then there were the enormous trees, the green lawns, the stray cats and dogs that they would take in and name. They had everything their wonderstruck eyes could possibly wish for. Most amazing of all were the nannies, whose love shielded them from everything unpleasant. The children all lived in and out of ten different homes, they would constantly drop in on one another then vanish like a puff of smoke, only to be found again in the oddest of places. *Where's Lucien? Where's Kate? Romane's vanished. We can't find Mackenzie! Anyone seen Rachel? Is Henry at your place?* The adults had no way of knowing where their children were, but no one ever worried because of the guards who stood at every entry and exit point along the perimeter of the complex. Nothing too bad could happen as long as they remained inside it. Free to roam, and with this heat, this pool, these friends, these animals, with all this love and laughter, the children might well have thought they were living in paradise.

Embargo

Post-embargo children would say, this was what Hà Nội was like in 1996, this was Hà Nội in 1998, in 2000, 2002, and all the other years, too. We met her when she was half-formed and wild; we grew up in step with her; and when we finally left she was regulated, vertical, and connected. In the space of ten years, from 1995 to 2005, the city transformed, evolving from a village girl with dirty feet to a city-dweller with ill-fitting shoes. Hà Nội carried us, her children, on her back throughout all these changes. We were there for ten or fifteen years, just the time it took for her to metamorphose. We were the last to see and know the face of twentieth-century Hà Nội. And, having feasted on her vibrancy, we, the post-embargo children, ended up leaving her for France, Australia, Canada, the United States, Italy, and elsewhere.

These expatriates did not belong to you, Hà Nội, so they left you. But they were crazy about you. And maybe it was precisely because they knew they would leave you that they were all the more eager to make the most of you while they could. They had seen you during those early years—the pure, true, visceral you. You were their penniless, loving, adoptive mother.

All roads led to you, no one could deny that. We, the children, were happy there with you, and none of us have ever forgotten you since. *Remember what it was like? Just seeing our faces from back then gets me every time. I can't forget you, Hà Nội.* Yes, that's what we say. Some of us even got tattoos of the country's silhouette—not out of patriotism, but out of some other feeling entirely. We weren't raised to idolize Hà Nội, we were raised *by* her. We were protected by her, loved by her. I say this and I believe it, the city was a mother to us. And you were my friends. All of you who lived there with me, you were my days: Mackenzie, Kate, Isobel, Jooen, Sharon, Yasmin, Romane, Rachel, Ngan, Henry, Duc Anh, Maxwell, Luca. I really do hear your voices when I stumble across your few, precious sentences from the four corners of the world. All these different names from across the oceans. We loved one another. It could have lasted a lifetime.

I for one genuinely believed that it would. That's what the conversations, the smells, the laughter, the routines, the faces— everything around me—promised... I thought that I, too, would grow up and get onto my little Honda and set off, overtaking other motorbikes, that life would be a party, that it would always be hot and we would always love one another, surrounded by friendly faces. I thought that I would grow up with Cô Phái and Bà, that I'd laugh, I'd yell, I'd be happy with my friends and my animals, that I'd find love there... I really did picture myself weaving through the streets on my motorbike for the rest of my life like my nanny, like my aunts, like everyone else. That was what I wanted. And then all of a sudden, none of it was possible anymore. Everything suddenly fell silent. All the noise stopped and the color drained out. The world fell apart.

One afternoon, without warning, the house was cleared out, our belongings tossed or packed up, our childhood pets—cats, fish, and tortoises—given away. *Who wants Kitty?* Everything disappeared. Cô Phái helped with the final tidying, Chú Tú helped with transporting things, the second H packed bags, and the young French man carried the heaviest loads and oversaw the work.... Once the house was emptied and locked up, the adults joined the two children and their friends, who had convened in the courtyard outside 501 Kim Mã. Bà and Trang and the other two H sisters rushed over. Picking up a camera, Chú Tú asked the adults to sit down with the children on their laps. His cigarette dangled from his lips as he pressed the shutter. Cô Phái hugged the little girl to her, the bitterness in her smile still visible in the photos to this day. Neighboring children clustered around the carousel, posing for a few grinning snapshots. Photos were taken with the grandparents, the aunts... I didn't really understand why. Were we making memories in advance? Was that like cooking food for later? Were these the very last photos we would ever take? Was this a goodbye? Why was everyone here, all grouped together in this courtyard on this particular day? It felt like the closing credits of a film... Was this the end? Yes, it was. The presence of the grandmother, the three sisters, the nanny, the children, the grandfather, the driver, and the father confirmed this. Everyone had gathered to say goodbye.

Hà Nội could have lasted a lifetime. We could have grown up with her. We could have known her when she was a rebellious teenager in the 2010s, as she covered herself in fast fashion retail stores and irregularly shaped tower blocks. We could have watched as she looked with envy towards the United States and wished she could be a bit like New York; as she looked longingly towards China and wished she could be a bit like Hong Kong; as she failed at both because she was still so scattered and chaotic. We could have felt half euphoric and half disappointed alongside her. But no, we never even got to know Hà Nội 2006. The young French tourist, who had by then been living in Việt Nam for fifteen years, decided it was time to go back to France. It was time for him to go home. And perhaps, in the end, this was a good thing. Perhaps leaving Hà Nội at that particular moment meant that our memories of her would remain achingly beautiful. Moving away in 2005 felt like leaving someone after ten years when the relationship is still strong and you're both still in love. Hà Nội will always remain in my heart as she was back then, filled with energy and enthusiasm in the aftermath of the embargo and the war that preceded it. She will always be a mother to us. We left her.

Just like that, the umbilical cord was cut. That afternoon, the young French man, the second H sister, and the mixed-race son climbed into a taxi that stood waiting outside 501 Kim Mã. The little girl climbed in as well. The driver was told they were going to the airport. Everyone else—the grandparents, the nanny, and the friends—remained in the courtyard. Photos had been taken, but you didn't know why or what they were commemorating. Was something about to happen?

You didn't realize it at the time, but something was slipping through your fingers. That waiting car, towards which you were being swept along with your bags, was tearing something away. The taxi doors open, and in you climb. Look, now you're all settled. The doors close. You turn around. You're just a little girl on the backseat of a taxi that's about to leave. Through the rear window, you can see Cô Phái on the sidewalk. She's waving a hanky and sobbing; your grandmother is crying as well. Two friends run behind the car as it draws away. As it gathers speed, the figures shrink into the distance.

The little girl smiles. She's happy; they're going on a trip. But why is everyone crying? No one explains, but her heart tightens slightly. *Where are we going? And more importantly, for how long? Why was everyone waving? What does everyone else know that I don't?* The figures behind them continue to shrink before disappearing altogether. The family glides along in a tide of traffic. The freeway, a strip of asphalt that offers the first and last glimpses of the city, cuts through rice fields as it flows inexorably on towards the airport. Straw hats and buffaloes scattered amongst the green stalks look like beige and brown dots. Two hours later, it's all over.

The plane takes off.

Hà Nội 2005. That heat is gone forever.

Thirteen years later, I stand facing 501 Kim Mã. Once the site of so much laughter, it's now a giant vacant lot... *What happened to the old residential complex that used to be here?* I ask a passerby. He tells me it was demolished at the end of 2005. Too much space was being used to house too few people, so the plan had been to replace it with a high rise office building. *And thirteen years later, it still hasn't been built?* I ask as I stare, amazed, at the empty space in front of me. It looks more like a deconstruction site than a construction site. The man chews on a piece of sugar cane.

No, he says with a shrug. *The project was abandoned. They tried to sell the land, but no one would buy it.*

Why not? This location is great! It's right in the center of the city.

But it's haunted.

What?

People say ghosts won't let anyone build anything here.

I stand there open-mouthed. This place where we used to play and laugh and swim—this home that had once been so full of love—is haunted? The man continues on his way, leaving me to contemplate the wasteland. I'm saddened at first, but then I feel a rush of euphoria. *It must be the ghosts of our childhood,* I tell myself. This might sound silly or naïve, but no more so than a site right in the middle of the city not being developed because people think it's haunted... What other ghosts could there be if not ours? No one else could ever be as happy as we were here, no one else could ever love this place as much as we did. And when we left, we took all that love and happiness with us. We *were* 501 Kim Mã. It could never be home to anyone but us. I turn away, disoriented. There's nothing left now except the snickering of ghosts. The lot is vacant, the past dissolved.

Old ladies

It's hard to know what the old grandmother, who had once nurtured an entire community under her roof, felt as she watched chunks of it break away. By the twenty-first century, Bà's family had shrunk to almost nothing. First her eldest daughter had remarried and moved to Poland, taking her two sons with her. Then her second daughter had left for France along with her husband and two children. This second, gaping hole had appeared next to the first, creating an indescribable void. Her house, once so full of noise, was now quiet. This old woman—who had stood up to beatings and bombings, who had fought war, famine, and childbirth—no longer had anything left to battle. She had defended her territory fiercely, but now two of her own personal guards had deserted her. Had everything she'd struggled for been for nothing?

Her combative character had created a mountain of loneliness, and now she was slipping down its muddy, unstable slope, her sadness creating deep grooves that further destabilized her sense of self. For a long time, she allowed herself to slide.

Then one day, her attention was attracted by a glimmer of light—

not something dredged up from her past, not a memory or an old resentment, but rather an object. Her curiosity was aroused by this shiny thing—so much so that she pulled herself out of her loneliness and boredom and went to investigate. What was it? A computer. Yes, what stopped her slide was the glow of a screen attached to a computer the size of a microwave oven. She spent days on end learning how it worked, then began making virtual friends and writing poems and controversial articles that she posted on a blog she set up for herself. Out of nowhere, a digital world opened up to her, one filled with lightning-bolt connections and electronic noises and shot through with blue, gray, red, and black. One beyond wars, lost daughters, and clay huts.

Bà was so captivated by the internet that we lost her to it. She even stopped calling her children. And to think she always used to complain: *Why haven't I heard from you since yesterday? You never tell me anything, you've all forgotten about me, you're so ungrateful...* That era was over. Now, if someone called her after a month's silence, she seemed reluctant to pick up the phone.

Is something wrong? Why are you so quiet? Is anything upsetting you?

No, no... she would reply in a breezy, faraway voice, *There's nothing to report... Anyway, I've got to go, I'm writing an article. Love you.* Then she would hang up and go back to typing away happily. She used the internet to say what she thought. Despite the regime's strict rules, she dared to speak out against it, sidestepping bans and frequenting activist sites. She became a militant blogger and enjoyed contributing to public debates. Her words spawned an outpouring of comments. She organized all sorts of illegal demonstrations with her internet friends, and often appeared at them wearing pink plastic shoes. Grabbing her handbag and scarf, she would run down to her scooter, and zip on over. The last one I remember concerned Vietnamese sovereignty over the Paracel and Spratly islands. The protesters raised their fists and carried signs and shouted for the Chinese to get out. And there in the front lines was my grandmother, a little flowery scarf around her neck. Nothing frightened her anymore. She'd already seen so much.

Arriving home in the evening, too exhausted to think about her absent daughters, she would log onto the internet and express all the indignation she'd shored up from a lifetime of experiences. She would also share her understanding of history, which she had loved so much as a schoolgirl. The internet was filled with people and noise; it replaced the public square of her childhood village. Though an old lady, she never gave up. Fighting was in her blood, in her heart, and in her bones. Goodness, how she could yell!

At sixty-five she fought her last battle. When she could no longer type, she stopped using her computer. The cancer that dulled her shouting and dampened her spirit was the only adversary she had ever lost to, but she did so with honor and pride. Everyone at her funeral wore white. The sisters held hands and cried. Wreaths of flowers surrounded her husband and daughters, her friends and her extended family. A breath of wind stirred the garlands, the white clothes, and the long black hair of the three sisters. Then it was over.

A group of youngsters in torn jeans with bleached hair and various piercings approached the mourners carrying a large wreath. They looked devastated. The sisters glanced at one another. *Who are these people? Are they family? We've never seen them before.* The sisters blinked back tears and burst out laughing when they saw the name of their mother's blog written on the wreath. Unfazed by the two-hour journey, Bà's fellow activists had come to the far-flung village where the funeral was taking place to say their goodbyes.

In the end, Bà left this world wreathed in flowers: the flowers of war, flowers from her daughters, and flowers from her blog. We can now hold her bones close to our hearts.

Yes, in the end, Bà returned to the village where she had been born. Her funeral took place in the cemetery that floats above rice paddies. She rests in the midst of all that greenery, not far from the pagoda in the middle of the lotus lake. Her black marble casket is surrounded by the peacefulness of fields and buffaloes and waters that reflect the clouds. Children run to the pagoda after their evening classes, their shouts rousing the sleeping mosquitos and the memory of the hard-working little girl Bà once was. Incense, flowers, a statuette of Napoleon, and cookies have all been laid on her tomb, alongside a portrait of her. Visitors pour water over the scorching stone as if it were a face, cooling it from the glare of the sun. The water evaporates instantly as the stone drinks it in. The wind sends shivers through the nearby leaves and sets the rice fields atremble. Bà's sister and one of Trang's brothers still live in the village along with their children and grandchildren. It remains a part of the family. Bà is at rest.

Sisters-in-law

The second H sister arrived in an unfamiliar city in her newly adopted country and immediately set about trying to integrate by looking for work. Meanwhile, she was also learning French, dealing with unfamiliar customs and affluence, and navigating an unfamiliar school system. She decided to take swimming lessons at the municipal pool as well, having never before had the chance to learn. On top of all that, she needed to get a new driver's license: her Vietnamese one wasn't valid in France. In Hà Nội, people would make U-turns in the middle of boulevards and honk furiously to avoid accidents. You had to plow into the fray with as much aggression as your engine would allow. *The road belongs to you, go ahead and drive on it. Don't let the assholes stop you!* her driving instructor in Việt Nam had explained. But that's not how things were done in France. And so she adapted.

Her husband's parents lived in a town near the city of Tours, as did his two sisters. Family gatherings no longer took place in a circle on the floor but rather on a sofa in the living room or under a chandelier in an elegant dining room. Meals were served with cutlery, cocktail picks, and special little forks for oysters. The second H acquired the roles of "belle fille" and "belle soeur" in her new French family. She also met her five French nieces and became a "tante." All the children, including her own, spoke French, sung French songs, and had French stories read to them. There was a lot she had to learn.

Because she was bright and inquisitive, she quickly figured out how to enter into this new story, how to adapt to these new customs. France in 2005 seemed so much further ahead than Việt Nam to her... 2005 was the year digital television was launched, Dominique Villepin was appointed Prime Minister, France was chosen as the site of an International Thermonuclear Experimental Reactor, and Laurence Parisot became the first woman to be elected head of France's largest employers' union. Riots took place in the banlieues and protests broke out in high schools... People in France, whether established, in the process of being established, or intent on challenging the establishment, knew exactly how things worked. They seemed so capable and mature in their fleece-lined coats. Compared to them, our lives in Việt Nam seemed clumsy and unsophisticated. We didn't have a clue about digital TV or political grandstanding. Instead, we walked around in the sunshine in our little sandals or sat half-naked in the pool with our friends. We sat on the floor as we chatted and ate, our minds numbed by a patriotic Communism as dull as a bowl of plain rice with none of France's sauces and trimmings. Her new country was another story entirely. In 2006, Amélie Mauresmo won the Grand Slam in tennis and became the talk of television. The first case of the bird flu was confirmed, politicians prepared for a presidential election, and the nation was gripped by the case of Véronique Courjault's "freezer babies," which children debated about on school playgrounds. Smoking was banned in public places, and major changes to personal income tax meant the loss of 7.5 billion euros in revenue for the government. Jacques Audiard won two César Awards for his film, *The Beat My Heart*

Skipped... The French were informed about everything, and outraged by all of it. They were always on the go, directing their attention at one thing after another. They themselves had willed their crises into being and they knew it. In Việt Nam, we ignored things, we just let ourselves be carried along by whatever was happening immediately around us. The third H sister, for example, had never heard of Hitler. When, aged thirty, someone told her he had massacred all the Jewish people he could find, she exclaimed, *Oh, what a nasty man!*

So there it was. In France, people had access to everything; the Vietnamese were still trying to secure basic necessities. The French were fighting against things we weren't even able to imagine. For the newly arrived young wife, it was all very abrupt. Việt Nam 1995 was coming up against France 2005, and she had to learn everything on the go. Without any reference points, friends, or mother to guide her, she was entirely reliant on her husband. She didn't know the first thing about France and its gray culture, she knew nothing about French neighbors or traditions or Sunday roasts, but in order to understand her husband's day-to-day life, she had to somehow cope with it all.

For her young daughter, only ten years old, moving to France meant not understanding anything, not saying anything, and not wanting to feel anything. In one blow, she'd lost both her grandmother and her nanny, the two women who had raised her, who had held her hand from the day she was born. She'd also lost her friends, her country, and her bearings. And in exchange for what? For the chilly silence of France, a home she hadn't chosen. And for a mother who didn't take the time to ask her baby 396, *How you're doing, my little one?* much less tell her, *You're beautiful, I understand you and you understand me, I'm listening to you, I love you.* In France, the two found themselves face to face, alone together as they'd never been before, yet the space and language and time for kisses and cuddles simply did not exist. In this country, the mother spoke less fluently than her daughter and so had a harder time communicating. She was more foreign. Cracks began to appear between them. The child didn't want to speak Vietnamese anymore. At school, when she was surrounded by other French children, she was ashamed of being Asian. She embraced being French, this nationality she'd been given. Her father's culture. Did she love it more? No, but she was determined to blend in, to disappear into this world that was so different from her past, from her heart, from the second H. This shift occurred easily and without much fanfare. Nothing tied child 396 to the second H anymore. Neither held on tightly enough to keep the other from slipping away.

They became strangers. Their differences were laid out for everyone to see: it was there in their skin, their language and gestures, their manners, the way they spoke. The second H, a stranger in a new land, had also suddenly become a stranger in her child's heart. This estrangement could very well become contagious and perhaps even fatal if not treated. It hid in the folds of their clothes and in the way they spoke to one another, creating a distance capable of drowning them in its cold shadow. It was driving them apart, but neither of them knew this yet. Nothing about it was overtly violent. It wasn't something they could touch or hold; they didn't even know it was happening. Only later, after the fault lines had already opened, did the shock waves of that painfully abrupt and definitive break with Việt Nam fully register. The girl grew up alone. How does war, exile, and fear stop someone from hugging their own child? I'm not angry about it anymore, I'm not asking for anything when I say this, I just need to tell you: *It hurts, Mom, it hurts so much.*

Why did we have to leave all those people? Why did I have to lose all that love? I keep asking these questions like a repeated sigh. It hurts. I loved them, too.

Cousins

France was colder than anything the little girl had ever experienced before. Everything sparkly and fun had been left behind, in Việt Nam. And for a ten-year-old child who can't picture a future involving airplanes, journeys, and reunions, "left behind" means something far, far away. When you're ten, if something is over, it may as well be broken. And it's true, in 2005, staying in touch was still not particularly easy: Skype, WhatsApp, Facebook, and all the rest didn't exist yet. So when the family arrived in France, it really did mean the end of her life with her friends, her nanny, her Vietnamese family. Her childhood had come to an end. The burning heat of Hà Nội, over on the other side of the world, was gone. Gone forever.

You had no control over any of this. You'd done what you'd been told, you'd climbed into that wretched taxi and showed that wretched ticket to the flight attendant, and as a result here you were now with no way back to Việt Nam, to your grandmother, to your nanny, to your five families and three mothers. Instead, here you were in this wretched, freezing country, wearing these horrible clothes, eating heavy food, and walking on these silent sidewalks. Turtleneck sweaters, coats, woolen scarves... What was all this? Never worn anything like it before. Minced beef, spaghetti, potatoes and cream... What was all this? Never eaten anything like it before. Pedestrians who waited for a green light before crossing, and cars that stopped meekly at red lights. Never seen anything like it before... God, it was all so boring!

Việt Nam had always been filled with so much movement, so much noise, shouting, and jostling. No one paid attention to the rules or the traffic lights; if you wanted to go, you just went. Scooters were always cutting each other off or making U-turns in the middle of the street; pedestrians were constantly plunging into the thick of it all, risking their lives. Everyone dressed in light clothing, they sweated in the heat, they were all constantly in motion... All this was lost to her now. She was stuck here in cold France, with its rigidly respected sidewalks, its civilized overcoats, its boring red and green lights: *Go on, it's your turn to cross. No, not now. Now.*

The house in France had been already been primed and was waiting for the little girl and her family, as if it, too, had been in on the secret. It came complete with wood floors and glass doors and mouldings, as well as rugs and paintings, wall-to-wall carpeting, and yellow kitchen tiles. A lace-edged green and white awning provided shade for the terrace where midday meals were served. Pots of roses and hydrangeas, flowers that did not exist in Việt Nam, surrounded a cherry tree planted in the middle of the garden. The cupboards were filled with cutlery and shiny cooking pots, and the bathroom featured Klein blue fixtures, a double-ended bath, and a shower with massage jets. On the top floor, the children's rooms had already been prepared with sheets on the beds. There were even a few cuddly toys scattered about. Everything had been made ready for their arrival.

A year earlier, anticipating his family's move, the young French man had bought the imposing structure on a boulevard in Tours. In the intervening months, he had lent the home to his sister and her three daughters. This meant that by the time you arrived, it had already belonged to another life, had already been filled with French voices and customs, had already experienced things that didn't belong to you: Christmas, French grandparents, winter clothes, mashed potatoes, cycling in the park. Juliette, Mathilde, and Joséphine had already crumpled their smell into the bed sheets.

Everything here was cold and clean and rolled along on pumped-up tires. In Hà Nội, doors and windows were meant to be left open; the house in Tours was closed up. It was meant to be a rock, a fixed, stable place in which to hunker down and take refuge. Rising up through four floors, it contained six bedrooms, an attic, a billiard room, and a wine cellar, and the children played throughout it, racing up and down the stairs from the basement to the attic. It was a vertical racetrack. Việt Nam was horizontal: all activities took place under the sun and in the yard or at the swimming pool. When people nipped off on their Hondas, heading out beyond the confines of 501 Kim Mã, it was as if they stepped out of the frame.

Here, the chilly stone house was like an ocean liner. No one ever went out: the young French man worked in his office up on the second floor, while the second H cooked and sewed and occasionally translated. The young French cousins who came several times a week were the only people who ever visited.

We had traded the chaos of life in a half-formed city for the comfort of stability.

The little girl, now exiled from everything she had ever known, immediately loved the three cousins who'd been living in the house before her. Well-behaved, studious, and fond of zip-up sweaters, they became her guides to France, introducing her to its customs. The girl learned about this new world devoid of shouting and excitement and pet animals by watching them. She told her cousins about her menagerie of tortoises, fish, cats, and dogs back in Việt Nam. She'd tried to rescue a small tortoise by smuggling it out in her backpack, and though it had managed to survive the long journey hidden in a cookie tin, it died a week after arriving in France. In the end, she hadn't been able to save anything. Việt Nam was over and done with and very far away.

She took refuge in her imagination, making up sun-filled narratives and writing little novels and plays in which her three French cousins acted. This kept all of them entertained and brought a little of Hà Nội's heat and playfulness into their lives. These performances, with their pretend stars and artificial sunlight, were the little girl's only pleasant memories from those first years in France.

At ten, she couldn't understand why they had left the paradise that was Việt Nam to come here to all this grayness. She didn't understand what it really meant to say goodbye forever to a family, a mother, a country.

Something began to die inside her. Overnight, she fell silent. What was there to say? *Where is everyone? What are we doing here?* There was nothing she could say, nothing she could love. The stories she dreamt up gave her somewhere to express herself, and the new French cat she adopted gave her something to love. But these were just a child's feeble attempts to soothe herself.

All of the excitement and enthusiasm the little girl had shown back when she lived at 501 Kim Mã were little more than a memory that survived thanks only to her imagination. She pretended to be cold and French, she wore zip-up sweaters and let herself be led through the streets, through the hours, and in and out of three different schools. She changed buildings and friends every year without flinching. Nothing belonged to her here in France, not even her feelings. All she truly possessed was her silence. Her childhood exuberance was a thing of the past; she had to make do with the smallest of flames to keep herself warm.

And a low-burning flame is not enough for a child who's been cut off from her country, her nanny, her grandmother, her friends. It was as if everyone had died in an instant, and in their place two French aunts and five French cousins had appeared, bringing with them other habits, other stories, other bones that did not belong to her. She'd lost all her points of reference, her sense of warmth and security. She had no one to talk to. She was just a girl waiting alone on a bench in her heart, her legs dangling over its cold slats. What was she waiting for? She didn't know. Being a child, she never thought about going back. She suffered without hope, without thinking. This bench in her heart, carved out just for her, had been there from the moment she'd been conceived. It was her assigned seat, one that belonged to her. And so that's where she sat. That's where she always sat. In Việt Nam, she had from time to time invited other people to sit with her on this bench: Bà would hunker down across from it; Cô Phái would sit down on it to her right; friends would sometimes prop their elbows on its backrest... But in France the only ones who visited her there were her cousins, and soon there was no one at all. So she sat there on her bench alone. Waiting. And when you're just a child, and you're waiting, and no one ever comes, you eventually give up.

December 30, 1995 had been a good time to arrive like a bomb in Hà Nội, into its post-embargo streets, into its love, into the welcoming arms of her nanny. But in chilly France, December 30, 1995 held no particular significance. This baby who had come along by accident on December 30, 1995 meant nothing here.

Field of honor

In 2007, French television began running commercials from retailers, France's first female presidential candidate displayed her bravitude on the Great Wall of China; the writer Julien Gracq died, as did the humanitarian priest Abbé Pierre, the Resistance hero Lucie Aubrac, and the mime Marcel Marceau; the presidential election campaign pitting Nicolas Sarkozy against Segolène Royal had everyone chanting "Sarko, Sego!"—a rivalry that may have rhymed but wasn't pretty to watch; rock star Bertrand Cantat was released from prison for manslaughter, stirring new debates about his guilt and kindling remembrances of his victim, Marie Trintignant; Sarkozy succeeded Chirac; speeches, agreements, and disagreements proliferated...

The little girl moved with her family from Tours and into an apartment in Paris. Her aunts and cousins evaporated into the chilly air along with the make-believe sun that the young girl had manifested through the sheer strength of her imagination.

She'd already changed middle schools three times in three years, yet here she was again, having to tackle new streets and attend new schools and encounter new faces that peered out at her from their turtleneck sweaters. Her world had collapsed out from under her once before, and now she had to find her footing again in new and unfamiliar terrain.

Paris was beautiful, with even more pedestrian crossings, more red and green lights. Paris was foreign. Paris was a battlefield.

Third war

Teenagers

Everyone keeps talking about a past that isn't yours, that you don't understand. Everybody else knows all about Marcel Marceau, Lucie Aubrac, Julien Gracq, even Jacques Chirac and French politics. This isn't a child's disconnect, it's a cultural disconnect. You are twelve and trapped in the gray, tangled, sunless maze of a France in crisis, a mess that isn't your own. You've lost your mothers and your country, and no one has bothered to ask how you feel about any of it. It all happened so quickly. And there you are, completely alone in the middle of it.

The young girl stopped smiling.

She is sitting on her bench as the Paris snow falls. Ice encroaches over the slats. She's waiting for her world to come back. There's a good chance it never will. Something about being here makes her feel like she's being dragged back to that moment when the decision to keep her or not was being made. She'd escaped then, but now here she was again.

I won't lie. The coming war was inevitable. Her childish efforts hadn't been enough; the games and warmth had vanished. So, like all the women of her family, the girl went to war. Not an external one, like the first war with the Japanese and the French, or the second war with the Americans. This war took place between one part of her and another. Yes, a war broke out inside her—a third war that would, like the first two, leave behind destruction and grief.

It started with famines and the sound of constant explosions. She no longer said or enjoyed anything anymore. She no longer felt anything anymore. Wave after wave of bombs had stripped her mental landscape of tenderness or love. Any future she might have imagined for herself collapsed, its clay walls caved in. All that remained was an endless war. One side roared on and on about crime and death and suicide, while the other buried its head in its arms crying, *Leave me alone.* The noise was overwhelming. And, as I've said, there were famines. One side was violent. To make sure no one could eat, it took away all provisions and burned them. Not even a single grain of rice was left behind. She turned away from sandwiches, cakes, and cheeses. *Die, die.* The second side was fragile. At first it suffered from this lack of nourishment, but then it got used to the way things were. In the end, hunger did not even register anymore. The first side was too angry to think about food, and the second side was in too much pain. Besides, other things needed to be done: there were bombs to counter or endure, zones to defend or relinquish. The girl was fifteen when this war broke out. It destroyed her.

Other girls were going out and gossiping, laughing, and talking about clothes. They had friends, boyfriends, parents, cousins, brothers, sisters, enemies. All she had was this war in the pit of her stomach, the cold of France, and the wasteland that was left in the wake of retreating memories. She was visibly losing weight. Her hair and nails stopped growing. No one was able to intervene in the fierce fighting taking place within her, but everyone could see it was killing her.

Each day, she would navigate narrow sidewalks and brush past gray walls on her way to high school. All the teachers and students noticed how anemic she'd become, her face little more than bruises, bones, and shadows... Some walked past her without a word, others taunted her. On Mondays, Tuesdays, Wednesdays, Thursdays, and, depending on her schedule, certain Fridays as well, she would sit in class, sad and silent. None of it made any sense.

I exiled myself to the back of the classroom to avoid everyone's stares. That's my memory of high school. As I listened to the teacher from my dusty corner, where empty desks were topped by upside down chairs, I would secretly read or draw or write. The other students discussed Parisian love and French life. They laughed about school gossip, engaged in idle chatter or serious debates... For them, my sadness was unfashionable. But I couldn't join their conversations. I had no idea what they were talking about and nothing to contribute, and it wasn't yet time for love. Death was shadowing me; I was utterly alone. So as soon as school ended, I would go home to read and draw some more.

Nobody seemed to understand what it was like to have a country and a mother right there, pressed up against your skin, for ten years, only to lose both in a flash with no explanation and no hope of reprieve. It felt like a kind of death. She was starting to worry the people around her, but no one breathed a word about this to her. In fact, no one talked to her at all anymore; it was as if they were afraid or ashamed of her, or just no longer interested. Everyone had deserted her. She'd become a country within a country whose population was killing itself. No outside forces dared to intervene. If they tried to send out a few reconnaissance helicopters, the troops would fight them off. With this war in her belly, she couldn't talk, couldn't stay, couldn't live with anyone anymore. She was dying in order to lose the little that was left. Time passed. The fields were laid bare. Her heart beat more and more slowly, winding down like a neglected watch. She had no strength left; as her soldiers battled one another, they became weaker and weaker. Soon she couldn't walk, couldn't go down the stairs in the Métro, couldn't make it back home anymore. Her bones were screaming, the pain in her knees was unbearable. The end had come. The war inside her had been lost. She was dying.

It all happened so quickly. In the span of a few months, your war wrecked your body and ruined your health. You had no appetite for anything anymore. You stopped eating. Nothing made you laugh anymore. You were no more than a child, a faded flower whose petals had been torn off. And you had stopped smiling. *She loves me, she loves me not.* No one remembers now, but back then your face was skeletal and disfigured. Oh, how it screamed death and pain. Anyone passing you on the street would know: this girl is dying.

One day, as she stepped onto a bus, a stooped, wrinkled, old lady stood up and gently nodded towards her seat. The girl shook her head at the absurdity of this, but the white-haired woman, who must have been near eighty, insisted. And so the girl acquiesced, sitting on the fold-down seat even though every bump in the road bruised her. By then, she was already pretty much fucked. Things were getting desperate.

Another day, she was standing in front of a painting in a museum when a security guard rushed over. The girl watched as the guard ran all the way from the other side of the room to her side. Had she stepped too close to the painting and inadvertently touched it? Was there something else she'd done wrong? She was getting ready to apologize when the woman took her hand and leaned in so close that her curly hair touched the girl's cheek. *Come with me, sweetheart,* the guard said. *Come, you need to sit down. I can put a chair next to this painting for you. Would you like that?* The woman led her by the hand. The girl didn't understand what was happening. *Are you okay?* the woman asked. *You need to eat something, my lovely. Look, I always have something on me!* And she'd opened one side of her jacket to reveal a small, wrapped hamburger wedged inside her pocket. The girl laughed at the sight of it. The hamburger was literally "on" the woman. It was almost like a joke. *Would you like it? Here, take it.* The guard held the hamburger out to her. *No, no thank you,* the girl said, still laughing. *Take care of yourself then, okay?* the woman said as she stroked the girl's cheek. *Your life's important, your health, too. Take care of yourself, little angel.* The girl headed into the next gallery still smiling. But the further she walked, the more she wanted to cry. This woman, like the old lady on the bus before her, had actually seen how close she was to dying. Which made her death all the more real to her. Yes, she would in fact like to sit down. And no, stop thinking that... Stop showing me that... What? Yes, I guess I must be dying... Her eyes clouded with tears. The paintings in the next gallery no longer existed for her now. It was all so sad and absurd. This angel was genuinely interested in looking at the paintings, yet she was going to die because she refused to eat.

She walked through the rooms of the museum one by one, wondering if death might be waiting for her at the end of a corridor with a chair for her to sit on.

Who are these people? What do they want from me? Why are they staring at me, talking to me, helping me? Where are the people I love? And where the hell is this anyways? Why am I in cold, cold France? Who am I?

She was a body destroyed. She no longer had the strength to go from one bus stop to the next. Her head spun, her legs gave way beneath her, she found herself unable to breathe. Her field of vision shrank. She could only see what was directly in front of her, everything beyond that was blurred and hazy like a distant mirage. Her hearing had also deteriorated. Nothing worked properly in this war-torn organism. And then there was that constant feeling of coldness—yes, she remembers the cold... She had goosebumps all the time, her lips were purple in summer as well as winter, in wind or in sunshine. She felt frozen even in the Balearic Islands, where they spent the month of August. She could no longer move properly; she couldn't walk, talk, listen, or see; she was cold and in pain. Her only respite from her suffering—the only place where she found shelter from her emotions and her incessant thoughts—was the bath. She could stay in the tub for hours, her bony body curled up in its amniotic embrace. Pinching her nose, she would stay underwater for minutes at a time until she almost passed out. People would knock on the door—*Line, open up, are you in there? Answer me, open up*—but she was oblivious to it all. When she would surface at last, allowing herself a breath, the cold would wrap itself around her lonely body once more.

And so she sat, all alone on that bench in her heart, her legs clamped tightly together, her arms crossed in front of her. She was waiting for death. She wanted it to come quickly. Cold and illness closed in over her, rain fell and the wind blew—and through it all, she waited. But the love she needed never arrived. Hà Nội was so far away it had vanished from her past; her tomorrow had become so compromised it could no longer exist in any future. And so she continued to wait, her body reduced to bones. All she had left was the here and now of her tiny self on that bench—legs clamped, body shivering, arms crossed—waiting to die. She waited and she waited. She had inherited bruises, she had inherited bones, she had inherited death. But love never arrived. She was fifteen.

Women

The second H's experience of the family's arrival in Paris had been altogether different. Here was a woman who'd once sheltered in a bunker under a bridge, who'd walked through the Moscow snow in sandals, who'd seen cooking pots melted down for five đồng and six xu. She'd known what it was like to sleep on a mattress even before moving to France, and when she was younger, she'd even tried pizza. So Paris didn't seem that strange to her. She fit in quickly.

But despite her success at learning the French language and familiarizing herself with French customs and sartorial codes, she still could not understand her own daughter. Why had this child of hers exploded like a grenade whose pin had been pulled? The family didn't know what to do with her. No one had ever really understood this little girl who'd arrived unexpectedly and without a proper welcome. She'd popped up out of nowhere, making everyone laugh with her jokes and whims, her funny faces and moods, her tacky tiaras and artificially flavored popsicles, her made-up stories and sparkling eyes. She had never seemed to need anyone but herself, so although she had invited people to join her on that bench in her heart, no one truly could. A mischievous child, she'd made everyone laugh right up until she herself stopped laughing. No one had any idea what to do with this ghost in their midst. What to make of her sudden insurmountable pain, her utterly transformed face? How did she end up on such a terrible, steep, singular, strange, and dangerous path? What do you say to a child who's become so distant, who's allowing herself to die? How was anyone supposed make sense of it all?

No one could grab a hold of her. She was slipping through their fingers like wet soap that once made pretty bubbles but has now fallen to the floor, its broken pieces skittering across the bathroom tiles. How strange to have brought an unplanned life into this world and watched it grow, only to watch it die against your will. How strange for a child to no longer want to live, to choose the embrace of death rather than the life she'd been given.

The rest of the family lived in the here and now, so they were unable to understand why this was happening to the little girl. They all knew that they were in France, that they'd moved, that everything was new, that they would have to adapt. They'd never experienced the essential, vital love that the little girl felt for the country they had left behind.

The second H spends her days learning French, math, and other school subjects... She's studying to be a school teacher. She commutes morning and evening, taking the train from Paris as she heads off to teach in elementary schools all across the region. She lives now in an apartment in the Fifth Arrondissement, a world away from the mud hut of her childhood. She's eager to take in all the shops and museums and exhibits and movie theaters and restaurants... She enrolls in dance and sports classes, and eventually gives up on the idea of being a teacher because the commute is too taxing. Instead, she works as a translator for several different companies, then as an expert witness in the Paris Court of Appeals. She likes going from place to place, from project to project. Her innate curiosity results in her spreading herself thin. She is the second H, after all. The sister with the smooth hair. The intelligent, observant, inquisitive one.

The first H, curly haired and impetuous, has also made a life for herself, but in Poland. She now has long, painted fingernails and careens through the streets of Warsaw in an enormous car, her two sons strapped safely in the back. She's still as spirited as ever. Having inherited her mother's blogging tendencies, she writes inflammatory political commentaries for newspapers. Her outspoken articles denouncing and opposing the regime have gotten her banned from Việt Nam. She's no longer allowed to return, which means she no longer gets to see her father and her youngest sister. She insists she doesn't give a damn, though she sometimes curses and punches her steering wheel. She stands by what she wrote; she was right to speak out against those dictatorial starched shirts in Việt Nam. *So they're throwing bloggers in prison these days? People are being banned from the country for calling out the government for being total assholes? Does freedom of the press mean anything anymore?* She honks her horn. *Why doesn't the guy in that tin can up ahead get a move-on already!* Did someone say "spirited"?

Gentle and easygoing, calm and impassive, the third H also stays true to herself. Unlike the impetuous first sister or the inquisitive second one, she's chosen to stay in Hà Nội. She lives in the same apartment where they all grew up, living there with her father and her only daughter. She remains there even after her mother's death. Every morning, she gets on her Honda scooter and goes to work. She comes home again for lunch with the family. Then, after an hour-long nap, she returns to her nearby office. After work, she comes home to prepare the evening meal. Sometimes she squabbles a bit with her daughter, who is a few years younger than the other grandchildren, and who never wants to drink the water that's been warmed for her. She ends her day by watching television or learning English after putting her child to bed.

These three women were now living three different lives in three different countries. They navigated the streets of Warsaw, Paris, and Hà Nội by car or by foot or by scooter, their hair curly or smooth or frizzy—H. H. H. in three corners of the world. Their childhood was what it was, but in the end, they remembered it fondly. They had been happy back then. And as they went their separate ways, embarking on separate adventures, life began to open up for them. Their worlds were expanding.

But no one could ever have imagined this: that the little girl—the first granddaughter—might very well be dying. Not knowing what else to do, they prayed and lit candles to St. Rita, the patron saint of lost causes.

The second H had never witnessed an illness as personal and devastating as this before. She was familiar with the destructiveness of war, but not the intimate, internal violence of whatever conflict was taking place inside her daughter. It was something she couldn't comprehend or control. Who could? Her dying child made her feel confused and distraught. Trying her best to understand, she talked at length to her sisters and her husband's sisters, who suggested she seek medical advice. Something needed to be done.

State of emergency

How could a fifteen-year-old who lived in a country as safe and prosperous as France be harboring such an unrelenting war within herself? How had this battle to the death with herself even started? It was unimaginable. Yet there it was. *Mayday! Mayday!* her face screamed wordlessly. In the end, help did arrive. When nurses from the hospital finally came to collect her, they did so with the same urgency and sense of duty that American forces had displayed in Normandy when they stormed St-Aubin-sur-Mer. Sword Beach, Utah Beach, Gold Beach, Juno Beach, Omaha Beach. Her city, her parents, her nanny, her grandparents, and her friends had all been stripped from the ruined beaches of her heart. The doctors had been sent in to rescue the only survivor. She was no longer conscious of who she was or what she was doing. She was both the patient and the disease. And so a state of emergency was declared. She was hospitalized in order to help her survive the war she was fighting with herself. She no longer had mothers, a past, love, desires. Could the doctors restore any of this? No. Would they even try? She lay unconscious on that white bed, waiting for someone to administer even just a small infusion of love into her veins.

Nurses

A whole year would eventually pass there in the hospital—long enough for her to reconcile with herself and come back to life, if not necessarily to good health. That would be asking too much; that would come later.

Before she can even begin to imagine rebuilding the collapsed walls of her physical body, she needs to build up enough sustenance and rest. A healthy body requires energy and enthusiasm. For now, her body is still Hà Nội 1945—a far cry from 21st century Hà Nội with its glass towers and luxury boutiques and cell phones and brand-new BMWs and English mixed with everyday Vietnamese. But even 21st century Hà Nội lacks traffic lights; its veneer of progress can't hide the fact that it remains slightly chaotic, backwards, loudmouthed, and poor.

By this point, she's lost so much weight she can no longer stand on her own two feet. With nothing to fuel it, her pulse has slowed and her blood pressure has dropped as low as her core temperature. Her body is threatening to give up; her head is already gone. She's a wreck. The only possible hope of restoring what's been damaged is to keep her in the hospital. *We'll take care of her,* the doctors say. And so she stays.

All around her in the hospital are other children on the verge of death: children who are sad or sick or marginalized, who've taken too many drugs, or eaten nothing, or eaten too much, or tried to take their own lives. Like her, the only thing they know is their own suffering. Assigned to different floors according to what ails them, the patients drift about like wordless ghosts in a hospital that's made up of white tiles and green glass and silence. Peacefulness surrounds them. They're here to be loved. They're children after all.

What do you do every day?

Not much. We're here to get better, the girl explains.

What happens in the morning?

We have breakfast in the cafeteria. That's always stressful. Then there's a daily medical visit to check our vitals—pulse, weight, heart, blood pressure, etc... After that, we have drawing classes or group therapy or some other activity.

Then what?

Then we go back to the cafeteria for lunch, followed by a long afternoon nap. After that, there's one last activity, then dinner and sometimes a movie. The nights go on forever.

Is it boring?

Not really. We do the same thing every day, but it's not particularly monotonous or boring because we don't need to think about anything. Plus, it's not like there's anything else to do. We're led by the hand through all our meals and activities. For me at least, that's more than enough. It's not like I'd sign up for anything else even if it were being offered. The only thing I'd rather be doing is reading poems. Or dying.

Don't you ever want to go outside to walk around, maybe get some fresh air?

No. Walking is still too difficult for me. I'm too weak. And anyways, people are always either staring at me or they're too scared to look at me. So, no, wandering around Paris is not my idea of fun. The only thing I enjoy is reading. Novels and poems allow me to forget. When I'm reading, the rest of the world disappears. Then I don't have to remember this shipwrecked body of mine. Then there's no one to point at it or look it up and down and judge it. Reading fills my time and gives me a sense of peace.

So you're not bored? Really?

In the hospital? No. Well, okay, maybe it can feel a bit stifling. Everything's always the same here. So it would be nice to see the outside world every once in a while. But all of us know that being out in the real world means being in pain. We'd be cold and frightened out there; we'd break. So the hospital rooms are more than enough for us, even if they are a bit sterile. In here, we're treated like children; we have no will of our own, no power, no resources. We're fed, cleaned, and housed. But bored, no. We don't feel anything, and we don't want anything. The outside world is just a distant dream. It's as if we're already dead. Do you understand what I'm saying? Is that what it means to be bored?

The only patients on her floor are girls between the ages of twelve and eighteen. The nurses hold them up and help them navigate the unpredictable river of their illness on a raft that keeps rocking back and forth. They weigh so very little. The smallest of eddies is enough to rattle their bones and can easily throw them overboard.

So that's what it's like at the hospital. For right now, she doesn't really exist—she's just a moving shadow without a body or a voice or needs or desires. Or a life. It's too easy to die. It's too easy to stop playing; all you need to do is unplug. It's too easy to die, we're hanging on by so little, so very little. *Young ladies, are you ready? Is everyone here? How are you doing today?* She's surrounded by other floating bodies. Some drift about, their eyes haunted, their heads nodding without understanding. *What the hell are we doing here? Not here in this room, but here, now, in our lives? Ready for what? No, we're not ready. There's nothing we're ready for.* And yet we're not dead. Here, in this waiting room, no one is dead. That's for certain. But no one's alive, either. That's just as certain.

The squeak of wheels startles them out of their stupor. A nurse is pushing a cart filled with tubes, a blood pressure monitor, a stethoscope, needles, and IV drip bags. The smell of disinfectant and medicine trails behind him. A few ghosts clench their jaws shut, frightened. *Good morning, girls! How are things? Ok, who shall we start with? Come on, you, why don't you go first.* The girls line up one after another like sickly foals: exhausted, terrified, and spectral. They're suffering, but they're somehow hanging on; they're hurting themselves, but they don't feel any pain. They want to die, but they're still alive. They want to live, but it's as if they're already dead.

Ok, you're the last one. Come on, sweetheart. The girl on the last chair is reluctant to offer up her arm, but the nurse takes it firmly anyways. She gives in. He straps on the blood pressure cuff and presses the pump once, twice, three times, then five times, then ten, going on and on until the girl's limb turns blue and disappears, engulfed by the inflated sleeve. Eventually he stops pumping and checks the reading. His eyebrows go up. *Oh my!* He unstraps the cuff—*All right, I'm done. Thank you, girls. Take care!* The nurse leaves, the wheels of his cart squeaking off once again down the corridor. The frightened girls give each other sideways glances or avoid eye contact entirely. Now that the foals have been left alone in their stalls, they can breathe again and relax.

This is how they spend their time, watching the days slip away, watching themselves slip away. They slide along the corridors from one activity to another and from one check-up to another until they wind up in the lounge, an area designated just for them. This hangout spot is a place where they can huddle together and talk amongst themselves. The nurses never disturb them here.

Some read, others study or do homework. Some of the girls bury themselves in glacial silence, lacking even the strength to move their lips. Others speak quickly, loudly, haphazardly, using words that don't make sense but that pour forth from their thin lips, their assertions colliding with negations, their happiness with their sadness, everything pitted against everything else, their adjectives and adverbs overlapping or crashing together. The truth is these girls are completely lost, though they don't know it yet; they think they're asserting themselves, but in fact they're letting themselves die. No wonder their words come out all wrong.

Sometimes the patients fall asleep here in their little lounge, their heads resting on one another's shoulders. An occasional kiss might escape onto a forehead, or a hand might stroke someone's hair. Deep down, they understand one another well enough, though they aren't able to do anything for each other. Measures have been put in place to prevent friendships. Sometimes the nurses have to take them aside to warn them that they're getting too close to someone. It's important that they avoid accumulating too much sadness, that they don't drag each other under.

Once, when I was allowed a long period of "leave," I wrote to a friend in the hospital whom I'd been told was doing poorly. She was one of the most artistic and sensitive ghosts I'd met while there. I was worried, so I mailed her a letter full of encouragement and drawings. My friend replied, and we started a brief correspondence. But it didn't last for long. A nurse from the hospital came to warn me that I needed to cut myself off from the hospital. My friend and I needed to love each other like sick people do, from afar. Getting to know one another too well would only make things worse. It was unhealthy for two sick people—two dead people—to love one another. I understood, and because I understood, I quarantined my love for my friend the way I had quarantined myself from my body and my life. That's what being at the hospital was like.

Parents

No one lives in this limbo but children. Is this a beginning? Is it the end? They're hard to make out, these gliding ghosts who wander up and down the hospital corridors day and night. They're black shadows against cold walls, angels with transparent bodies. Their white gowns, from which an elbow or a bone occasionally protrudes, trail along the floor, their hems worn thin and fraying. *Tap, tap*—go their frozen feet wrapped in cotton as they walk across the floor tiles. It's too late for hugs, for being held. The only things embracing these shadows now are drugs and drips. It's simpler this way.

Parents are allowed to visit during the day, the cadence of their steps as they slip through the halls or lumber along completely different from everyone else's. The sounds they make—their heeled shoes, their anxious conversations, their jangling handbags and car keys—in a word, their lives—cut through the silence. *I mean, really, can you imagine... Honey, where are you... What room was it again? What floor? Wait... No, listen, the doctor said that, not me! No, we have to do what he says, follow his instructions... Do you have any news? Fuck, I left my card* downstairs, I'll go back down... I'm so worried, darling... You be quiet! Don't talk to me like that. Look... We haven't seen each other for three months, we can't start by fighting... It's not working... Open up! It's not working, I said... Just pull it! Push it! We're late, oh, sorry, ma'am! The ghosts listen in wonderment because they have no feelings left. They're no longer capable of anxiety or conversation or laughter, much less shouting or outbursts. They've gone completely numb. Even the sentence "Fuck, I left my card downstairs" is something to envy because it references a whole other life. The ghosts, meanwhile, don't have cards, can't go downstairs, and they definitely no longer have any fucks to give. Nothing about their day-to-day life excites them. They're dulled by pain.

So when the parents show up, hoping for news of their children, the contrast is stark. Parents come in all flavors: divorced, frantic, irritable, helpless, reconciled, gentle, tearful, optimistic... They're colorful, too, with their coral blouses, blue jeans, green jackets, mauve suits, turquoise scarves, purple umbrellas, white shoes... Whether scruffy or chic, boorish or pretentious, inadequate or over-the-top or just right, they're all visitors from life, carrying with them the smells of the Métro or a car or a motorbike or a hint of rain or wind or noise. Still, one way or another, they all end up in that same waiting room, distraught at the sight of these lives they created that are now so close to death. They eye the other parents as if to say, *You too? This is so painful, isn't it? It's such hell... Yours? Yes, mine too...* But they never talk to one another; they're too discreet, too polite. Too distressed. The doctor, a bespectacled face above a white coat, half-emerges from his office and says: *Mrs. So-and-So? Please come this way.* He beckons with his finger. The mother stands up shaking, her heels clacking against the floor, her keys clinking against her handbag, which she clutches with all ten clammy fingers. She enters the office. The door closes behind her.

When their parents leave, the children watch them return to their cars from the wide hospital window above. The sight of their parents walking down streets and disappearing around a corner makes them sad sometimes. Other times it makes them angry. Oftentimes, they're confused about how to feel. The parents are the first and most essential emissaries from a life the children no longer understand, that they've forgotten. And so they wait.

The young French man and the second H never imagined they'd end up here, side by side in a room in the basement of a hospital, waiting for news of their sick daughter. The possibility of this child dying before them was one they'd never imagined. *Had they missed something? What could they have overlooked?* they ask themselves as they sit, hand in hand. *Sir? Ma'am?* They're called into the doctor's office. They stand up and walk toward whatever verdict is about be pronounced. Someone else will be making decisions about their baby now. She no longer belongs to them anymore. They no longer have any say in her fate. Did they ever? Her future is no longer in their hands.

The doctor frowns, concerned. He props his elbows on the desk, joins his hands, and rests his chin on them. His glasses slide down his nose. The parents sit facing him. His eyes are hidden by the light from a desk lamp, which reflects off his glasses. They lean forward, their backs stiff, their faces anxious. Their hands are clasped.

What's going to happen to her? Has she stopped growing?

The doctor nods. *Yes, her bones have suffered severe trauma and calcified... She won't grow anymore.* It's hard to say whether that's a tear gleaming behind the doctor's glasses or just a trick of the light. The parents stifle a sob.

She's fifteen, she can't have stopped growing.

I'm so sorry, says the doctor, *Her body will remain that of a child...* Her parents squeeze their hands together even more tightly. After a while, they ask another question.

What about children? Will she be able to get pregnant? Or is that all over for her as well?

The doctor is afraid it is, yes. *People often don't realize that this illness can cause sterility.* She won't grow anymore, and she will no longer be able to have children. As small as she is now, that's the size she's going to stay.

If she won't grow, and if she can't have children, will she at least live? That's the question they're desperate to have answered. They want to grab the doctor by his collar and howl and shake him until his glasses fall off: *Will she live?!*

Let go of me... I don't know!

There's a pause as the doctor picks up his glasses and puts them back on his nose. They're a little crooked; they might be broken. *Will she live?* The question, asked again softly, so softly, slices through the silence. Nobody has any strength left. No one knows how to reply. *Will she live?* None of this is anybody's fault, nobody knows what to do, no one knows how or why all this began. And now the girl will always remain a child, a child who'll never grow, who'll never have children, who'll stand alone on the earth without a past, without a future, without the life her parents had imagined for her. She's broken, but there's nothing anyone else can do about it. She has to figure it out by herself, to save herself, even if she can't see any reason to do so. It's like learning music without any notes. How can she be made to understand that she has to stay because she's already here? What can be done to make her want to do so?

Her father wishes that he knew what to do, that he could find some way to help her. But he doesn't and he can't. He's not the one dying. He no longer has any control over what's happening to his daughter. She's no longer the pretty, chubby-cheeked, mixed-race child she used to be. She no longer smiles, no longer looks like a little girl; she's not expressive in any way. This person who should be his daughter is instead the very image of death, a skeleton sailing across the waters and into another realm. He doesn't know what to do anymore; there's nothing that he can do. The situation is slipping through his fingers. Horrified, he falls to his knees and bends over his little girl's motionless body crying. She's just skin and bones. He feels a hand patting his shoulder. *Everything's going to be okay*, the child's voice says. Exactly which part of this is going to be okay? This river that's flowing too fast? This hand like a bundle of bones that's patting my shoulder? This voice whose cold scent already belongs to the past? *Tell me—yes, you, Death, the one who is trying to reassure me, who's touching my shoulder to console me even though you are the very cause of my pain—how are you going to be okay? How will any of this ever be okay?*

Children

What is it that the girls on this floor of the hospital have seen? What have they been through? What have they lost that makes them want to keep on losing so much more? Something inside them must have come undone for them to be so intent on undoing what remains. *I'm going to finish what I've started,* say the bones that poke from under their skin. Who started it? How? Why? These girls are fifteen, sixteen, seventeen years old, they're on the verge of becoming women. But because they refuse to move forward, they've remained children. They're moving backwards to disappear, rewinding to their starting point in order to erase what lies behind them. They sit there, these girls, mere skin and bones, as if to say *I'm stopping, I'm not going any further down this path you've chosen for me. I'm done.* Nobody says anything, nobody knows anything, nobody wants anything. There's no one left inside these bones.

Children? Yes, children. What I see in that hospital are children, children who refuse to eat at mealtimes, who don't want to do what they've been told. In the canteen where lunch and dinner are served, the patients are constantly being urged by the nurses to chew and swallow. Isn't this absurd? No, it makes perfect sense that these girls don't want to eat. This isn't about dieting or being picky, it's about something much more vital than that. Having already lost so much, they're deliberately trying to lose everything. Which is to say, having left life behind already, they have no choice but to get to whatever's on the other side. Their faces, their bodies, their bones, all clearly state that they don't want to live, that someone or something has already killed them. But it takes a lot of work to get from here to there. So offering food at this point is just rude. In the face of so much pain, steak and mashed potatoes are an insult. What's so important about chicken or a chocolate bar when pain itself is so vast, so noble and essential, so inevitable, so criminal? Food interferes with the hard labor of destruction. The main course and dessert on the meal trays they refuse to finish represent life and death. Food or death? What's at stake here is not whether or not to eat dinner. It's a question of living or dying.

The girls are suspended in limbo, they haven't yet chosen which way to go. No one in this hospital knows what the ultimate verdict will be—not the nurses, not the suffering girls themselves. No one knows whether or not they'll make it, and more importantly, who or what is going to determine the outcome. That's the big question. It might very well be up to the kinds of decisions the girls make for themselves every day. Could it be that the answer lies on this very tray of food? That's the worst part: the choice of whether to live or die might be right here on this tray.

I'm reminded of the pig being slaughtered under the table by nurses who were in such a festive mood that they forgot the urine samples, those birth certificates in waiting. Bon appétit.

Today, at twenty-three, I'm making this trip back to Việt Nam to gently turn the page on that teenage version of myself. I'm making this journey so that I can give her an answer, one that's not just for her—for me—but also for a family that can no longer sustain a story built on fractures and fault lines. I'm coming back in order to understand why baby 396 felt she had to die. Why her and not baby 395 or baby 397? Why did you beat yourself up so badly, little girl? And what gave you the courage to come back from the brink that night?

Yes, I'm talking about that night when you came so close to dying... And when I say "so close," I mean the very border between this life and the next. You reached it, the ticket counter of death. Remember, you were very sick, not by your own doing, but with the stomach flu or something, one of those nasty viruses that makes you throw up. You got up in the dark with that taste at the back of your mouth urging you to throw up, it was rising up inside you, it had to come out. Teetering, you made it to the bathroom, closed the door, and knelt on the floor. You crouched over the toilet bowl, your bony knees creaking against the floor tiles, your bare legs aching. The water waited motionless in the bowl. You were about to throw up; a lake of sulfur or scalding pitch was roiling inside you. But there was nothing there to throw up, you'd lost everything already—your height, your stomach, your weight, your flesh, your body. It was all over. You felt nauseous and needed to throw up; and if you did throw up, that was it, you would die. You remember. I remember. I can't forget your emaciated face, my emaciated face, can't forget how you died, how I died, how the two of us held hands over that toilet, you, the broken little girl who was prepared to die, and me, who'd do anything to make you better.

I'll remember that night in the bathroom for the rest of my life. I had no breath left in my lungs, no energy left to fuel my beating heart, no flesh on my bones, nothing... If I had thrown up right then, I would have died, there in front of that toilet. And one part of my body begged me to do so: *Go ahead, throw up! You feel sick so throw up! The* other part of my body refused: *I can't, you know I can't, if I puke now, it's all over, I'll die.* I'm dying. I'm going to kick the bucket here in the bathroom because my heart's beating too hard, my lungs are wedged up against my stomach, against this urge to vomit, and I'm about to die, everything inside me is all messed up, it's not what I want, I'm not the one who wants this... I don't want to die.

I managed to reach my arm out and flush the toilet in an attempt to scramble my thoughts and the timeline... I watched the water swirl noisily, knowing that if I puked, I would die. An hour went by. I managed to keep myself from throwing up. I swallowed down my suffering, breathed it in. My stomach dropped down low, and so did my lungs. Air trickled back in. The toilet water stayed clear. I could breathe again. My knees were now purple and blue from spending too long on the floor. But I was breathing, a thin thread of air, a saint's sigh, a fairy's cry... I went back to my bed. I hadn't died; but I'll always remember that frontier, my eyes rolling in the dark, in the emptiness, my eyes that could already see themselves crossing to the other side in that toilet bowl, that swirling water.

So, little one, you stepped up to the ticket counter that night, and when the woman handing out tickets looked you right in the eye and asked, *Are you taking one?* You hesitated. You asked whether it was round-trip and could it be returned? The woman looked you up and down and said, *One-way only.* She held the ticket out as if to say, *Given the state you're in, it seems like your time's up. Just jump already.* But the girl hesitated, there was still time for her to back out. She glanced over her shoulder: the river was rushing toward her, tumbling downhill, its waters spilling over, churning, its eddies filled with dark blues and clear blacks, with foam and death, all of it underscored by thunderous noise. She either had to take the damn ticket or face climbing all the way back up. But she was so thin, so small, so all alone.

Of course you're heartbroken. By destroying yourself, you destroyed everything—friendship, family, love. But by then you were already too dead to figure out how to save anyone or anything. You're heartbroken because you made everyone around you cry. Even so, it was still possible for everything to start again, right? Everything could still get better? Those were the questions that your eyes—the last part of you left alive— asked of your scrawny body.

Families

The young French man and the second H now lived in an apartment on the second floor of a modern building that housed about ten other families. The building was not particularly distinctive, but it was a clean, practical place to live with all the usual amenities: elevator, automatic lights on the landings, parking, basement storage. Their apartment, with its central living room and seven small rooms connected by a long corridor, contrasted starkly with the house in Tours, with its carpets and mouldings, its many floors and beamed attic space. Lacking a garden, greenery, lakes, wandering animals, and children from different households running in and out, it also differed from the residence at 501 Kim Mã. No, in Paris, things were arranged vertically: people lived between four walls on a single floor of a multi-floored building overlooking a street, a distribution that isolated inhabitants behind closed doors. Back in Việt Nam, doors were always swinging open: anyone could come in to ask, *Is my friend around?* Because there was nothing to steal, there was nothing to fear. Doors were never locked, and people were always being invited into homes and offered tea. When they moved to Tours, this habit continued with their cousins, who would often drop by without warning; after all, it had been their home too. But the apartment in Paris was sealed up. Just getting into the building required having a code, then a second one, then the interphone, an elevator, a landing, a doorbell… Dropping in on anyone casually became impossible; everyone just stayed in their own homes. Meeting up meant agreeing on a time, and schedules were always tight: *Shall we have dinner on Tuesday the 21st? No, I have a meeting then… Oh, well, how about Thursday the 23rd? Ummm, two weeks from now? That works for me. Send me your address and the code.* The only way you would hear from people was by telephone. The real voices— those childhood voices that used to call up from under your window, *Line, where are you? Me and Rachel are going to the pool! Louis's on the carousel with Henry!*—now came in from somewhere far away, isolated and disembodied, over crackling telephone lines that often cut off. *Sorry, I don't have any signal.*

As we moved from Hà Nội to Tours to Paris, there were fewer and fewer voices and space retracted into itself. The abundance of green in the residential complex in Hà Nội, with its lake at the end of the park, shrank down to a cherry tree, a patch of lawn, and a couple of bushes in Tours. By the time we got to Paris, all that was left was wooden flooring that never changed with the seasons. Our homes got smaller and smaller, too, the white walls of the bedrooms drawing in close, the beds shrinking from a full-size to a twin to a single. I remember the day I was shown my bedroom in Paris. *Do you like it?* I made a face. For someone who loved wide open spaces, this was a cage. We were accustomed to running through the streets, to the grime of Hà Nội, to seeing certain faces, faces that didn't exist in this place without animals or cousins or nannies.

That long dark corridor leading to seven rooms was like a Métro line with seven stations. My mother would get off at the first stop, her bedroom; my father at the second, his study; my brother at the third, his bedroom; and I would alight at the last stop. Opposite these were three communal stations: two rooms for bathing and one toilet. No one ever went into anyone else's room; everyone had their own personal area. That's just how it was.

The young French man forbade his wife and children from disturbing him while he was working in his office. And he was never not working. The only difference was that now he spent his days writing at the second station along that corridor instead of outside or on another floor. The second H had room where she worked, too. And like everyone their age, the children never allowed anyone into their bedrooms.

I feel anxious whenever I think about that dark corridor that ran through the middle of those rooms. I used to walk along it every day during my depression and anorexia. Whenever I was allowed out on leave, I would visit the second H and the young French man and walk down that corridor with its hospital-white walls. Wanting to cheer me up, my father decided to paint the doors different colors: pink, blue, green, yellow... He was willing to do whatever it took. The results made us laugh for a few weeks, but nothing really changed. His daughter was still sad and sick. She would sometimes smash her forehead against the wall of the small, square room at the end of the hallway that felt like a cage, banging her skull against the mirrors until the glass shuddered and almost broke. No one knew what to do.

When she came home, the smell of her anguish would seep out from under her door and into the hallway, accompanied by the sound of her head hitting the walls. The young French man, the second H, and their son came to dread her visits. She never came alone; Death was her constant companion. The two were a frightening sight to behold as they trailed from room to room, or cried on the sofa, or shared a family meal, or lingered motionless and stagnant on a chair... The family no longer knew how to react to her. They felt threatened and overwhelmed. Their attempts at encouragement washed up against a wall of steel. Their humor, their smiles, their anger: none of it worked.

They must have resented her for giving Death a place on their sofa, in their living room, at their dining table. Their entire apartment reeked of Death, this presence that caused their apartment to slump its shoulders in defeat as it started to crumble under the smell of a sadness that never seemed to leave. Death had the keys to their apartment: it arrived before the girl and lingered on after she left. Its very presence asked questions of the three residents. They found themselves unable to talk; words could no longer ease the immense distress they felt when faced with the girl's destroyed body. Even the brother no longer understood his sister. He could no longer bring himself to hug her. No one could touch the girl; she was unreachable. Everything became impossible: her relationship with other living beings, her love for life, her joy, her conversations with friends and parents, her ties to her brother... Nothing could survive in that darkness.

The family's helplessness and bewilderment grew as the girl continued to decline. The terms used by the doctors were foreign and incomprehensible to the mother, as was her daughter's pain. It was frustrating. The father, shut away in his study, threw himself into his work, both as a way to escape and because it was his duty. The brother didn't know where he fit in, which side to take, or what role he was supposed to play. Still just a teenager, he was an innocent bystander. Like his father, he worked hard. Though he got brilliant grades, there was nothing he could do for his sister... All three felt powerless.

Unable to act and incapable of understanding, the family felt paralyzed and helpless. This both pained and irritated them. When it was just the three of them, they could talk amongst themselves, ask each other why this was happening or what they should do. They could say to one another, *I can't take it anymore, she's killing me, too. I don't understand. Why is she doing this? Why?* But as soon as the girl arrived, arm in arm with Death, silence would drive them apart again. They could no longer ask her anything. Whenever they did, she would dissolve into tears. She refused to accept advice or anything else from them. So in the end, all they wanted was for her to go away. Because she wasn't going to get better. Because her illness was too contagious, her war too destructive. What, after all, can be done for a country in the grips of a civil war? Anyone setting foot in it is likely to be bombed. The only solution was for her to go back again to the hospital. That way she could be alone with Death once more. Death was her first, her most painful, her most passionate, her most destructive relationship. Her greatest love. Death filled the hours of her day, it was her anguish, her abusive lover. Between Việt Nam and France, between the child she had been and the woman she would become, between accidents and choices, Death stood there—dark, impenetrable, unavoidable. It was her secret lover, her special perfume, her torturer. Death was her reason for no longer being.

Girlfriends

2012: Putin is President of Russia, Hollande of France, Morsi of Egypt.
We witness several solar and lunar eclipses. The Olympic Games take
place in London and, from outer space, Akihiko Hoshide launches the
craze for selfies. Hurricane Sandy destroys parts of the United States.
Neil Armstrong departs from this world, as do Oscar Niemeyer, Chris
Marker, Whitney Houston, Antoni Tàpies, and Donna Summer.

Why is it that I can never picture a face when I say a word that's so
common, so easy for others—"Mom"? Why was I born feeling so alone?
Where were you when I was growing up? I know you were navigating
foreign languages, exile, social classes, customs, battles of all kinds. But
why did I have to suffer so much in your wars when they weren't even
mine? Others had ocean views while I only had a view of death.

My hospital window looked out on a line of trees planted in grey
sidewalks filled with strangers. When I first arrived at the hospital,
aged fifteen, their naked branches were covered in snow. Soon the
warmth of the sun melted the ice away and covered their branches
with spring leaves and new buds that the heat of summer would
turn into petals before autumn winds stripped them bare again. The

brown branches shivered under the ochre sun, knowing that they would be covered in snow before long. Yet hidden buds were preparing themselves to bloom once more.

Seasons passed. I bandaged my wounds with white pages to hide a pain that was increasingly difficult to contain. I swathed my agony with a thin ray of love that covered an endless sadness. I wrote. I made myself smile with poetry. I read to escape. I ate. I forced myself to do whatever was necessary. Like Trang, I sheltered under a two-sided roof, but mine was made of reading and writing. I traveled in my imagination. Time passed. I took care of myself. I made a point of staying warm and bundling up. I wanted to get better.

I was beginning to recover physically. Once I forced my body to accept nourishment, my organs began to function again. The strike was coming to an end. My heart continued to beat, my stomach digested, my lungs breathed, my liver cleaned my blood. Little by little, the engine came back to life, its temperature rising. My head was still thudding against the walls, but I was out of the woods physically. Because I was no longer in danger of dying, the hospital decided to liberate me. I could go. Someone else was already waiting to take my place.

So I went back to that Paris apartment. Every second of every day was a struggle for me. I struggled to go out, to talk, to eat, to see friends. To live. But I always had my books. They were my window onto the world. Everything I read—novels, plays, poems—was an escape for me… I traveled through historical periods, experiencing the adventures and emotions of different characters in costume dramas, tragedies, and comedies. I also went by myself to art shows. The paintings spoke to me. I recognized a pain akin to mine in the works of artists I admired. Activities like these provided me with an internal escape route, a way to live and love outside a world in which I was dying and felt unloved. These were enough of a temporary reprieve to sustain me. I went back to high school as if nothing had happened and applied myself with a passion born of despair. Little by little, my shrunken field of vision began to open up again, its blurry edges coming back into focus. I noticed well-intentioned faces, friendly smiles, endearing jokes. I made friends with Palmyre, Lola, Victoire, Gabrielle, Salomé, Clémence, Shandiva, India... Precious names with upstrokes and downstrokes and long, generous curves, that I carefully arranged in a circle around my own thin, stiff, short, broken one. Line. Four little lost letters pronounced in an abrupt syllable. This Line—this moon, this glimmer in the dark—was as evasive and distant as the night, ready to die in order to avoid being seen. My friends were the sun. I clung to their long, warm days: Palmyre, Clémence, Gabrielle, India, Salomé, Victoire, Lola, and Shandiva.

Want to grab a coffee? Or see a movie this afternoon? Ok, let's meet at Odéon tonight. Hi! How's it going? Oh my god, I need to tell you what happened with François... Ok, you'll never believe this... How about you, how are things with you? No, come on, forget it, people were standing in line for like an hour, we'll go some other time. Meet us at Vic's place. I'm so screwed, I'm losing it, I'm gonna have to lock myself in and study for the next ten days... If you don't hear from me, I'll be drowning in flashcards... Hey, Shandou, chill... Breathe... Do you prefer me in pink or blue? The blue looks better on you, Gab. Amazing... So are we going to Italy this summer or not? I can't wait to be with you guys, lying in the sun in our swimsuits, talking, drinking good wine, I love you guys so much... Come on, Line, move it, fuck, she's always like an hour late, it's driving me nuts... Can we meet at the Tournelle Bridge? There's something I gotta tell you... You ok, sweetheart? Yes, I'm meeting Palm, how about I catch you later? Yeah, call me. Love you.

My friends were happy, intelligent, gentle, patient, understanding, funny, warm, and loving. Like the characters in the books I read and the actors in the movies I watched and the muses in the paintings I viewed. They brought so much life back into my world. During my convalescence, I filled my often solitary days by discovering things I had never experienced in Việt Nam or Tours: red velvet seats in independent cinemas, multi-colored exhibits in magnificent museums, black cigarettes and white coffee (or the reverse), bouquinistes and their thousands of used novels. I forced myself to feel the warmth of these Paris sidewalks that had always seemed so cold before. And then there was high school. We were now seventeen, eighteen, and all anyone ever thought about were their crushes. We talked about them during breaks, passed around notes in class... I, too, played at this game of crushes, and was lucky that a few boys were interested in me, though everything was always more talk than action. Still, love, even when just pretending, was already living.

The second H, relieved that her daughter was healthy again, went back to her various activities. The young French man shut himself away behind the painted door of his study and labored relentlessly over vast amounts of work for the sake of his family.

Then there was my brother, my almost twin, so close in age yet so far apart. He'd had a hospital in Blois, a springtime birth in April of 1994, and a mother prepared to receive him. Meanwhile I had been an accident, with neither a mother, nor Blois, nor the month of April. Instead, I had Hà Nội and December 1995 and, most importantly, the scent of death, which followed me everywhere. This brother, who'd been hit by a ricocheting bullet from my civil war, exceled in his scientific studies and went on to join the army after graduating from school. A lieutenant in the Foreign Legion, he paraded under the flags of the Champs Elysées on July 14th and would later join the special forces during the 2015 terrorist attacks. He wasn't even twenty-three yet. Were all his forays into battle his way of standing by my side as I fought my own war? That answer is not mine to give. All I can say is that he has more than proven his courage and his tenacity.

The seasons kept changing. It was inevitable that the war inside me would come to an end at last.

It was time for me to take my final exams. While in the hospital, my schoolwork had been a lifeline. I'd kept up my grades and never been held back, so getting my diploma was no trouble at all.

After that, my horizon shifted. Everyone else kept talking about how to orient their careers, their plans for the future. But my body, my heart, my inner compass were all pointing in the same direction. I could imagine only one path for myself: a return to Việt Nam. Alone.

Ceasefire

It's impossible to imagine ever escaping the dampness of a thick, motionless cloud when still caught in its cold shadow. It happens, though. One day, a ray of light breaks through... At first, the relief is only temporary, a moment of warmth, a scrap of sunshine within a nimbus of darkness. These brief spells are never enough, their light paler than that of Hà Nội's—less complete, less maternal. But they do exist. And we need to learn to notice them, to hold on to them fiercely so that they can save us.

What is there beyond this life? And is it worth it? Having died, having gone all the way to the other side, do you just decide one day to come back? Why? What for? Everything here is so cold and fucked—the planet, mothers, life. Everything's already over and done with and none of it will come back. The most we can hope for are these pale rays of life. Are they worth the effort? Yes. Even if there's no good reason to go on living, even if there's no way of knowing what will happen next. And the thing is, perhaps nothing will happen. But it's important that we continue nevertheless. It's true that coming back and staying is going to be horrible; every single day will be a battle. But things are already horrendous. Even when Phoebus doesn't shine, we have to love him all the same. There's no obligation to remain, no love that's keeping us here. We've already lost everything. Yet we have to stay.

You never imagined life was going to be like this: existing as a body, organs, bones, as a first and last name, being on earth for no particular reason, for no one, without love, without passion, without desires. Feeling like an empty carcass, but having to stay regardless.

Why? Just because. This is true of any struggle. There's only one battle that really matters, the battle to be human. There's only one kind of strength, only one kind of courage. You have to stay just because. What a pointless justification for such a vast mandate. And yet we play along; we obey. We have to stay because we're already here. This right here is what is meant by the word "God." There's nothing else. What I mean is, this is Life. This is just the way things are. More precisely, this is the way humans fit into the way things are. Leaving won't break anything you know, but it would take such courage to stay, to endure the suffering... So what will you choose?

You got better. You reclaimed the body, face, and thoughts of a living person. Death slipped out and the little girl returned. Now that you had chosen life, now that you were back and walking about, you decided to revisit your childhood—to see for yourself the places you had lost, those places whose loss had almost killed you. You were just barely seventeen when you flew back to Hà Nội on your own for the first time. And now, you see, I'm twenty-three and returning alone once more—back to the scene of your childhood. You came back and I'm going back again, too, following in your footsteps as always. Perhaps I'll never stop going back to find you, to find that girl who came into this world, the one who died, the one who kept trying to find herself. The one who wrote, who kept coming back. Perhaps I, too, will keep coming back to that little girl. To these different caskets of bones and the layers of the past contained within them.

2013

It only took eleven hours for the seventeen-year-old girl to find her way to the city. As expected, it was in good health: new glass towers had sprung up, and gaudy new luxury shops proliferated in 21st century streets invaded by growling BMWs and 4G cell phones... Hà Nội had a new face—one that wasn't hers.

The taxi took the road from the airport to the city. Despite the passing of the years, the buffaloes were still there. The rice fields, too. Even through the window, she could feel the humidity clinging to her skin. She hadn't felt it in such a long time. Crossing the Red River, the taxi glided into Hà Nội, slaloming between cars and motorbikes. It went down Kim Mã and turned off into smaller streets. The grandfather and the third H had bought a new house in a nearby neighborhood. The driver found his way through narrow alleys and came to a stop when he couldn't go any further. The girl slipped him a bill and took her suitcase from the trunk. The wheels on her suitcase raised clouds of dust as she made her way along a path that cut through a market with stalls of bún chả, cơm ruốc, and fried fish. What was this new place? She found herself stepping over troughs of water and avoiding hands, feet, chain link fences, and pots that stuck out into the street. Finally, she reached the gate. Here it was. She rang the doorbell.

Her grandfather opened the door. He stood before her. It had been so many years since she'd last seen him that they no longer spoke the same language and had forgotten each other's faces. His hair had turned white. He hugged her, and even this warmth felt strange to her. So this was where her grandfather and aunt lived; in this calm, five-story home that was far too big for them.

He gestured for her to come in, then offered her tea and fruit in the living room. They ate together in a silence filled with emotion, nibbling away at all the time that had passed. The taste of the chilled lychees was as cold and intense as the fluorescent lighting overhead. Hardly daring to glance at one another, they kept their eyes on the fruit as they spat the black, gleaming pits onto a plate. Trang, the teacher, sat facing his French granddaughter, this once little girl whose birthday was on the 30th of December just like his wife's.

Noticing that the girl kept blinking, tired no doubt from jet lag, the grandfather suggested she go rest for a while. They stood up. He explained that there were plenty of bedrooms, enough for all those who had once shared meals in a circle on the floor—not just the sisters who had left for Poland and France but also their husbands and exiled children, should they care to come back. Even Bà had been assigned her own room, one where they would go, bringing offerings of fruit and cakes, when they wanted to talk to her. *Where is it?* Up on the top floor. Her grandfather asked if she would like to go and pay her respects there before taking her nap.

She went up to the fifth floor. What was this she was feeling as she began climbing the stairs? Was it fear? These customs were so foreign to her now, this language and time so unfamiliar. A framed photograph of Bà was waiting for her in an otherwise empty room. Bà's room. She continued past the unused bedrooms, reminders of how much time had passed and how many people were no longer there. The stairs were steep, and there were so many of them. As she neared the fifth floor, she found her excitement strangely tempered by a sense of detachment. The only light in the tiled room came from a single window. A white curtain swayed in the breeze. Bà's photograph sat on a tall altar surrounded by sticks of incense and dried fruit. It was motionless like a solemn grandmother. Bà wasn't smiling. The girl recognized this grim expression, this face that stared straight into the lens. What was she supposed to do? Say hello? She hadn't been taught these rituals, didn't know if she even believed in them. And she hadn't spoken Vietnamese for such a long time. Everything about this house, this scene, was so foreign to her. But the words came nonetheless: *Chào Bà... Bà có khỏe không...* This broken voice belonged to both a child and a woman. It was still filled with death and exile, but it was grown up and alive. *Hello Bà... How are you...*

She made a habit of going up every evening right as the sun was setting to spend time with Bà's silent photograph. The shrieks of children faded into the growing darkness as the city settled. This was Bà's time. Then, using a precarious fold-down ladder, she would climb onto the roof and look out over Hà Nội through the canopy of criss-crossing electric wires that obscured the winding streets. It was only then—with the last faint sounds and smells of the day rising around her—that Hà Nội came back to her. Back as she remembered it, as she'd known it, as she'd left it. One floor below her, Bà, who'd been through so much and seen so many things, sat on an altar, her expression forever grim. Trembling with emotion, the girl would climb back down from the roof, close the trapdoor behind her, and pay her respects to Bà one more time. Then she would head back downstairs to where dinner was waiting.

Everything and everyone had grown up or grown old, starting with the city itself. She no longer spoke the language, no longer looked like she belonged here. The Hà Nội she remembered from her childhood didn't exist anymore. She was a foreigner not only in France, but here in Hà Nội as well.

One morning, she noticed a small, wrapped cake on the breakfast table downstairs and ate it without thinking. It was delicious. She was already showering upstairs when she heard the third H give a horrified shout that made her drop her soap:

Who ate the cake for the dead?!

Shit, that was Bà's offering? I should have known it was way too good to be for breakfast. I'm such an idiot!

The voices downstairs continued to deliberate: *Who would steal a cake meant for the dead?*

Do you think Line might have eaten it by accident?

Oh, yes, that's probably what happened.

It wasn't a big deal in the end, but the incident highlighted yet again how much of a foreigner she was now. Embarrassed, she hopped out of the shower, dressed, and went down to apologize. Yes, she really had eaten the cake for the dead.

A motorbike weaves its way through traffic, leaning dangerously to one side then the other as they accelerated past one vehicle after another... The girl holds on tight to the driver with both hands. The roads in Hà Nội belong to the motorbikes, and no asshole is about to stop them from getting through. The wind whips her face and hair as she rides this galloping steed to the address written down on a piece of paper clutched between her anxious fingers. She's on a mission. The bike comes to a stop at the corner of an alley. Thanking the driver, she gets off. This is the final stage of her pilgrimage. She continues on foot, making her way between stalls of noodles. She can't remember Cô

Phái's face anymore. All she knows is that her nanny is married now, that her husband drinks, and that she sells bún bò nam bô from her house. Will they recognize one another? She stops outside a house that, like all the others around it, is crumbling under the weight of stones and electric cables. Its number matches the one written on her piece of paper. She rings the bell.

A woman opens the door. Laughing and shouting, she pulls the girl into her arms and sobs. She's ecstatic, her eyes sparkling as she chatters away in Vietnamese, a huge smile on her face. Two young children come running out and throw their arms around their mother's legs.

Mommy, Mommy, who's this? they ask.

It's Line, darlings...

Who's Line?

Cô Phái shows the girl in and offers her a bowl of her famous noodles: *They really are the best on the street!* The girl accepts, and Cô Phái hurries off to fetch bowls, chopsticks, noodles, and grilled beef. Setting all of it on the floor, she tells everyone to sit down and eat. *How are you? My darling... Tell me everything.* Communicating in Vietnamese is difficult, so they talk in smiles as Cô Phái's children squeal, run around, and climb on their mother's back. *Leave me alone for just two seconds! Calm down, I'm talking to Line! You two are such a nightmare.* Lunch comes to an end when the grandfather rings the doorbell. He's come to take his granddaughter home. Cô Phái invites him in and offers him something to drink. He thanks the nanny turned best-bún-bò-vendor-on-the-street turned mother-of-two-nightmarish-but-gorgeous-children. Then they all say their goodbyes, and the girl leaves with her grandfather on his motorbike.

It's just a moment, nothing big. And now a motorbike is weaving its way through traffic but in the opposite direction. The girl holds on tight to her grandfather. She's no longer on a mission; her pilgrimage is over. Wind whips her hair and her face as her grandfather races past the other vehicles. She holds on tight to him, hoping he won't notice her tears. She's crying because the past is the past; because her nanny is older now and has children of her own; because the motorbike is racing along in the shadow of high-rises that she didn't get to see being built; because it's Hà Nội 2013; because she never got to see the city grow up; because she hadn't been there for Cô Phái and the children; because life went on without her. She's been alone all this time, waiting on her bench for someone that will never come; someone with a life of their own, separate from hers. The person who was supposed to show up has gone somewhere else, and she's still alone on her bench. She turns her head and leans deftly away so she can't be seen in the motorbike's wing mirror. She doesn't want her grandfather to see her tears because it would worry him, and he wouldn't be able to comfort her. She doesn't have the words in Vietnamese to explain what she's feeling. It's over. The love she's been waiting for all these years has taken another path. She stifles a sob as the motorbike enters the maze of streets around her grandfather's house. They're almost back. She gulps and is wiping the traces of salt from her face when bike comes to a halt at last. The grandfather turns to his granddaughter: *Ready?* She tilts a bright, dry face toward him and smiles: *Yes, let's go.* He didn't see a thing.

They go into the house together. Her grandfather switches on the television and settles on the sofa, and she goes up to the top floor. She lets down the ladder and climbs onto the roof. She's alone here. Hà Nội's rooftops stretch out before her, the sky wide and open. She'd waited such a long time for this reunion with Cô Phái, and she's suffered so much while waiting. But this mother isn't hers. Not really. She cried on that motorcycle because the tumult around her wasn't hers either. Hà Nội 1995 and Hà Nội 2005 are not Hà Nội 2013. The city is no longer hers; the mother she thought she could find here no longer belongs to her. She's all alone up here on this roof. She needs to come to terms with where she is and who she is beyond this rift, this absence, this void, this photograph of Bà on an altar. Now she knows: nothing is waiting for her here. It's over. Time to go back to Paris.

The taxi driver is waiting for her to climb in. He might even be the same one from before. But this time, she's the one who's saying, *I need to go to the airport.* She's the one choosing to leave behind these figures that are quickly fading from view. This time, she knows why they're disappearing. She's the one choosing to cross over the swaying bridge that takes her out of the city, to drive through rice fields dotted with buffaloes until the only place left to go is onto an airplane. This asphalt road is the beginning and the end, an unfurling red carpet that ushers people in and out of Hà Nội. And she's made the choice to leave. She's choosing to check in her luggage, to hand over her passport and her ticket, to climb onto the airplane, to go through the clouds, until she arrives in the cold of the country that is now hers. France is not the country where she was born, but it is where she lives, where she's choosing to grow up, to no longer be alone. She's no longer a victim of anything anymore. We're in 2013. She's seventeen, and she's going to find her own place in the world. Too bad for the husbands that beat their wives, too bad for the jealous women... too bad for the dead women and the ration tickets. Because that's the way life is sometimes. And she's no longer a child. She's going to find her own plot of land, one on which she can build herself a home to welcome a family she's chosen for herself. The plane lands. We're in Paris. There are no more victims. The war is over.

France 2013: the Champ-de-Mars is inundated by massive crowds of demonstrators; horsemeat is discovered in frozen beef products, causing consumers to once again question the rules regulating food sourcing; the French Senate adopts a new law on tax amnesty for corporations; Budget Minister Cahuzac is found guilty of fraud and resigns, resulting in calls for transparency; the Constitutional Council confirms the Assemblée Nationale's legalization of same-sex marriage; and *Blue is the Warmest Color* wins the Louis Delluc Prize for best French film. All these names and events suddenly mean something to her; they've become stories she remembers, connected to a place she calls home. Việt Nam 2013 is a place whose stories she couldn't possibly know. She was there from 1995 to 2004, and leaving it behind had been so very painful. But now, we're in France. This is where we live, where we've chosen to make a life for ourselves, building up this thin body, filling this gray life with color. We've chosen to understand, to look, to accept, to start over. We're not mere victims of dizzying upheavals—we know what's happening. We're not ten anymore. We might not have had a chance to finish being a child, we might have missed out on being a teenager... But now we're going to live on our own terms.

2018

There are so many difficulties to face between the waters of our birth and the bones we leave behind. We know—or at least have come to understand—that the reason we must stay is because we're already here. And so we stand tall, our feet in the water, caskets of bones overhead. We stand here for those who came before us and those who will come after us. And also for those who are still around us. We're here. We don't really have a choice. But maybe—just maybe—we can decide how we want to stay and what we want to be.

She understands now that she can't go back anymore, that she has to move forward towards whatever comes next. But alongside this road that stretches out into the future, there are also a multitude of other branching possibilities, paths that sketch the outlines of her demons and her dreams, and by so doing, her inner landscape as well.

The same is true for everyone else around her: the mother, the father, the aunts, the brothers, the friends, the cousins, the lovers. Each is ruled by the circumstances of their birth, their own primitive waters; each decides how they want to live, what they want to leave behind in their own casket of bones. They are all doing the best they can, each in their own way, and together they form a family of souls, one that walks together because they know that doing so is worthwhile, that the paths they choose will be beautiful, painful, breathtaking, that they will be filled with escape routes, scenic short cuts, wide boulevards, dead ends, steep climbs, breakthroughs. And that at the end of it all, they will always find one another again, at some crossroad or another. Always. This is what gives them the strength to forge on. There will be surprises along the way, people hiding in the bushes, other, fabulous things, and it's all worthwhile. It's important to keep on going, right to the end, together, with these waters and for these bones. Because although it may be frightening and filled with so much uncertainty, it's also beautiful.

A simple image makes you smile—that of Bà's funeral. The world won't remember this tiny woman or her small life with her small family in a small country. But her funeral was attended by neighbors from the village, cousins, friends from Hà Nội, her husband and her loving daughters and their foreign husbands and mixed-race children... not to mention those bloggers in their torn jeans. In the end, her funeral brought together Hà Nội 1945, Hà Nội 1960, 1980, 1995, and Hà Nội 2005... And that was sufficient. She had done so much, you see. Bloggers attended her funeral, France and Poland were in attendance, too. So yes, life is worth living.

Destiny is not a vise clamped shut. You can slip your finger inside and ease it open by the narrowest of margins, robbing it of its power. My story has not come to an end, as I once thought it might. And the proof is that I'm twenty-three, and I've come back to Việt Nam once more. I'll always come back. Because each time I do, things will have changed. This story will never end because it shifts year after year, taking on the form into which we've tried so hard and with such agonizing effort to mold it.

This summer, I step off the plane and leave my bags at my grandfather's house, then head out alone to try to get over jetlag by taking a walk. I tell him I'm going to be back in an hour. I don't think about where I'm going, I just place my trust in my infamous sense of direction and, more importantly, my feeling of belonging to this country, this city. *This is your neighborhood,* I tell myself. *You know it. This is where you're from.* I set out full of confidence, looking straight ahead so that no one will mistake me for a tourist. I try to melt into the crowd, walking as if to say, *I know where I'm going.* But the streets are so narrow. Everyone else seems to know each other so well, and there are so few tourists. My path twists and turns as I wander.

Soon, I'm lost in Hà Nội's backstreets, unsure which way to go. I feel helpless, almost in tears. My grandfather isn't picking up his phone. It's over 45°C and I've been going in circles for forty-five minutes like a stylus on a scratched 45 rpm. I'm drenched in sweat and ready to curse the whole country. I can't take it anymore. Night is closing in on these streets that I've circled forty-five times; everyone can tell I'm a tourist, that I'm lost. Trying to get back to my grandfather's house, I ask them if they know Mr. Mac and where he lives. No, no one knows. I set off again, still going in circles, still sweating. *What am I going to do?* Then I remember. It's my first day back in Hà Nội, but I remember.

I call Cô Phái. She picks up straight away and squeals, *Child, you're in Hà Nội? You have to come over right away! Here's the address... You can stay the night! Please come! I'm still at the market, I won't be home for an hour, but the kids are home... Just go in.*

I hail a motorcycle and ask to be taken to her address. The driver tears off along the main road, then turns down narrow back streets before dropping me off at last. I remember this maze that I navigated five years ago and am able to find my way to her house. There it is: one room, ten square meters, with a kitchen that spills out onto the street.

The door is open, of course. There might not even be a door.

Two children are lying on the tiled floor inside. They're eight and thirteen now. *Xin chào*, I say in my awkward French accent. Turning around, they both look up at me. Then the younger child runs over and throws her arms tight around my waist. *Line! Line!* How does she know who I am? Why is she so excited to see me? We only met that one time, during that brief, hazy trip when I was seventeen. But there's no mistaking her happiness. *Line! Line!* She continues to shout, jumping up and down before sitting back down on the floor to peel and cut up her mango. She's in charge of dinner. She keeps glancing up at me impishly, and her smile warms me. It's tender like love, like my mother's daughter, like a little girl, like a grandmother. It's strange, but I love this little girl the same way she loves me, with an indirect, diagonal bond.

Cô Phái sells backpacks now instead of the best bún bò. She goes to a different market every day on her motorbike, a giant bag filled with backpacks strapped to each side. All three of us turn around when Cô Phái pulls up and honks. *Chào cô! Chào mẹ!* we call out in greeting. She laughs and comes in to join us, kissing her children and pulling me into her arms. This time I don't hide my emotions, sobbing right there in front of everyone, even the children. You can't hide from life, so why bother with masks? Here I am in tears, stripped bare, and Cô Phái says, *It's okay, it's totally normal. Go ahead, cry.* She knows. She hugs me to her, talks to me as if I were her own daughter: *Do you remember? You were only a year old and I was twenty-three... Now you're twenty-three... Remember how you left thirteen years ago? Well, guess what, Chát is thirteen...* The children and I look at each other while Cô Phái looks away discreetly. The World Cup is on TV, and she lets herself be drawn into the game. I'm still crying, and my nose is red. Her son's playing with a plastic ball and yelling excitedly about how much he loves football and how he wants France to win, not Argentina. Cô Phái gets up and goes to fetch a box of Choco Pies. She hands me one. *Eat,* she says. I look at her. *These were my favorites... I know, I know,* she replies as if to say, *Of course I remember, what else did you expect?* She's been buying them ever since.

I decline her invitation to stay the night; my grandfather must be thinking something's happened to me since I disappeared into the labyrinth of streets more than four hours ago. After dinner, Cô Phái takes me back on her motorbike. I put my arms around her waist as we make our way through traffic. She turns her head and, through her helmet, tells me to hold on tighter. My hands are clasped around her, my palms against her skin. She knows. Everything that I'm feeling right now, she's feeling too. I cry openly, not trying to hide. *I loved you, I missed you, we were broken apart... and I was just a child.*

But I'm a woman now. I understand. But I know I will always come back. Even if there's no definitive answer here. This place is a knot I have to work out, a necessary stop on my way to anywhere else I might care to go. Maybe one day I'll come back with a daughter of my own, who knows? And maybe the time after that, she'll be thirteen, too, like your son is now, and I'll be forty-five, like you, and life will go on. And maybe she'll come back again, too, when she's twenty-three like I am now. Who knows? The wheel will turn, and we'll keep changing along with it. You see, you can find childhood fractures as well as answers in a nest. And this nest is alive. It's a city.

The plane is ready for take-off. The airport is filled with people and suitcases; as I look to my left, I can see them hurrying through glass corridors. The runway stretches out in front of us. Planes land and take off like white-hulled whales at the bottom of the ocean, their fins cutting through the air. Some are sinking down, others are floating up, enjoying this aerial dance between white clouds. The engines roar like animals. We, too, will soon be roaring off. A stewardess announces that we're about to take wing. I'm going back to France—to my country, to the language I speak. To my familiar gray world.

Sorry, excuse me, coming through. I grab my luggage. Airport taxis, grumpy Parisians, the beltway. Paris comes into view, its churches, its Eiffel Tower, its orderly streets and clean sidewalks, its red lights and cafes where you can sit and drink a coffee, its buildings where my friends and my lover and my family live. I'm a foreigner in Việt Nam, a foreigner in France, a foreigner in... But Paris, I know you. And you know me well by now, too. We've hurt each other a little, but you love me, don't you? Because I love you. Because there's life to be found here, too.

Armistice

So there it is. Each pallid morning during those violet years, I would wake up to a clarion call. A call to combat. Before I even stepped out of bed, hordes of enemies would already be massing below. It took all my strength just to open my eyelids and gather my courage to jump into the fray. It was war. I knew we were going to bleed and get knocked down, that we would end up injured and black and blue. The streets were our battlefield, the Métro our trenches, the bus stop our bunker. But the violence was inside me. I knew that each day would be an ordeal. You could never afford to drop your guard. You had to grit your teeth to want to live. I never had time to yawn or cry, I was always in danger of being taken out by a bullet.

Then, without knowing how, the mornings became brighter, changing from purple to lilac to pink. There was room now for a faint breeze, a sunbeam: a wink, a helping hand, a smile. They were just fleeting moments, but they were there, unmistakable, in the midst of all that war. The clarion softened. Mornings lightened to the color of cream, honey, wheat... The streets became friendly, the Métro calm, the bus stops quiet. The blood dried, the blows stopped, the bruises faded. Life was becoming easier. One day, the clarion sounded loud and clear again—but it wasn't calling for battle, it was announcing a ceasefire. The artillery had stopped shooting. I'd kept a little bit of the war inside me, so it took me a while to understand that an armistice had been signed. I didn't notice right away, but the sun was beginning to warm me. Yes. And life came back. As did love. We could still grow up, become women, live. We would love and perhaps even be loved. And we would be beautiful. We would become mothers, grandmothers, veterans; we would live no matter what. The mornings were the color of cream, honey, wheat. The third war had ended. The embargo was about to be lifted. Life could start again.

About the author

Born in Hà Nội, LINE PAPIN moved to France at the age of ten. She is the author of five critically acclaimed novels: *L'éveil* (2016, Winner of the Vocation Prize), *Toni* (2018), *Les os des filles* (2019, Winner of the Readers' Prize of Le Livre de Poche), *Le coeur en laisse* (2021), and *Une vie possible* (2022). She lives and writes in Paris.

ABOUT INK & BLOOD

Ink & Blood, a collaborative project between the Diasporic Vietnamese Artists Network (DVAN) and Kaya Press, seeks to introduce literary works capable of reconfiguring conversations about the Vietnamese diaspora. Drawing its name from a writing group that would evolve into DVAN, the Ink & Blood imprint spotlights politically engaged and formally experimental writers who are working at the limits of the diasporic imaginary.

ABOUT THE TRANSLATORS

Award-winning translator ADRIANA HUNTER has brought nearly 100 books to English-language readers and still enjoys the buzz of finding promising new francophone authors. Her recent work includes the international bestseller *The Anomaly* by Hervé Le Tellier and *Sapiens: A Graphic History* based on Yuval Noah Harari's global phenomenon, *Sapiens*.

LY LAN DILL has been translating for more than thirty years. She specializes in the humanities, notably colonial Vietnamese history and diasporic literature. This is her first translation of a fictional work. She would like thank Kaiah Callahan, Sunyoung Lee, and Austin Nguyen for their tireless efforts and support throughout the process of translating and editing this book.